TOM SWIFT AND HIS
ELECTRONIC RETROSCOPE

THE NEW TOM SWIFT JR. ADVENTURES

BY VICTOR APPLETON II

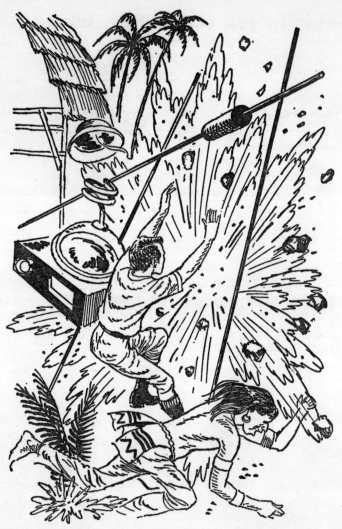

The rock absorbed too much radiation from the retroscope and exploded

THE NEW TOM SWIFT JR. ADVENTURES

TOM SWIFT

AND HIS ELECTRONIC RETROSCOPE

BY VICTOR APPLETON II

ILLUSTRATED BY GRAHAM KAYE

NEW YORK

GROSSET & DUNLAP PUBLISHERS

CONTENTS

CHAPTER I

MAYAN WELCOME

"THIS is a new kind of scientific expedition," Bud Barclay remarked with a grin, "bringing pygmies out of the Yucatan jungle!"

"A bit different from our space cruises," Tom Swift Jr. agreed with a chuckle. "Bud, these small men are not pygmies; just the shortest of their particular tribe of Mayan Indians. Doctors hope to learn a lot by studying them. For one thing, their pulse rate is twenty points lower than ours."

The eighteen-year-old, blond-haired inventor was flying a Swift cargo jet high above the Mexican wilderness. Bud, his friend and copilot, sat beside him.

A third man, Chow Winkler, suddenly said, "Bet my last grain o' cayenne pepper those pygmies won't come!" The chunky, bald-headed man, a former Texas ranch cook, served as chef for the Swifts' various expeditions.

Chow squinted out the plane window and shook his head worriedly. "We'll prob'ly end up with arrows in our backs!" he prophesied.

"Tom and I needn't worry about filling their dinner pots." Bud winked at Tom. "One look at a nice plump specimen like you, Chow, and they'll forget the rest of us."

"Y-y-you mean th-these Injuns we're lookin' for are cannibals?" The grizzled cook turned pale under his Western tan. "Brand my sagebrush stew, I should've stayed on home grounds back at Swift Enterprises."

Chow made his headquarters at the Swifts' huge, ultramodern experimental station. It was here that Tom and his father developed all their inventions.

"Relax, old-timer." Tom soothed the Texan with a smile. "Fly boy here is pulling your leg again. The Mayas are really a very fine and peaceful people."

"They ain't savages?" Chow gulped.

"Far from it. They're full-blooded descendants of the ancient Mayas who ruled here before Columbus, and built great temples."

"And practiced human sacrifice," Bud added with a mock-fiendish chuckle.

"Not any more," Tom said. "They are very happy people nowadays."

"The Mayas may be peaceful now, but there are still plenty of jaguars around." Bud continued his teasing. "And those big spotted cats can really be mean when they're cornered."

Chow grinned feebly. "Wal, I'll stay in my corner if those cats'll stay in theirs! Say, how long you figure on bein' in that jungle, Tom?"

"Only long enough to take on my passengers, Chow. I'd like to get back to my lab as soon as possible and work on the new camera." Tom had been developing a television-type camera which he hoped to use in restoring, photographically, ancient writing and carving.

After winging over the blue waters of the Gulf of Mexico, the Swift cargo jet had flown southward across the Yucatan Peninsula. Tom now consulted a map to find the Mayan village where they were to pick up the natives.

"Where can we land?" Bud asked, worried.

The terrain below was a dense green mass of tropical rain forest, with the shore of the Caribbean Sea visible off to the southeast. There appeared to be no spot to set down.

"Looks as if you'll have to use your new plane," Bud told Tom.

He was referring to another of Tom's amazing new inventions, which he had brought along for an emergency of this kind. The plane was part jet plane and part dirigible. After the dirigible's bag was filled with helium, so the plant could float without power, the bag could then be slowly deflated to bring the ship gently to earth.

Bud Barclay had nicknamed the craft a "parachute plane" or "paraplane." Tom hoped to perfect it to a point where disastrous air crashes would become a thing of the past. His first test model was stowed in the cargo hold.

"You're right, Bud." Tom spoke over the microphone to Slim Davis. "Report to the flight compartment!"

Cutting the main engines, Tom fed power to the jet lifters to hold the ship steady in its present position. Slim, a Swift test pilot, entered the compartment a moment later.

"What's up, skipper? We almost there?"

"The village should be somewhere below, but we'll have to use the paraplane for a landing," Tom explained. "Bud and I will get it ready. Take over."

"An' I'm comin' along," Chow declared.

As Slim eased into the pilot's seat, Tom, Bud, and Chow hurried out through the passageway and down a ladder into the cargo hold. The sleek little paraplane, its wings folded neatly into the fuselage, stood with its nose aimed toward the cargo hatch.

"How we goin' to float down in this contraption?" Chow eyed the strange-looking craft uneasily. "I thought it was s'posed to have some kind o' balloon or gas bag or somethin'."

"It has," Tom replied, "but the dirigible bag is deflated now and stowed inside this pod." He pointed to a domelike bulge on top of the fuselage. "We'll blow it up with helium as soon as we're air-borne."

"Wal, don't wait too long, Tom!"

As several crewmen stood by in the cargo compartment, watching with interest, Tom, Bud, and Chow climbed into the cabin of the paraplane. Tom took his place at the controls and adjusted his headset.

"All ready, skipper?" a crewman's voice came over the earphones.

Tom held up his thumb in response. The man pressed a button. As the door of the loading hatch slid open, all the crewmen hustled out of the compartment to avoid the paraplane's jet blast.

A light blinked on, signaling all clear. Tom warmed up the engine, his heart pounding. Although he had test-flown the paraplane back home in Shopton, this would be its first real tryout under different atmospheric flight conditions.

Chow gripped the sides of his bucket seat, pop-eyed with excitement. Bud Barclay flashed the young inventor a tense grin. "Here goes, pal!"

"You said it!" Tight-lipped, Tom flicked a switch to release the chocks and open the throttle.

With a mighty *swo-o-oosh*, the paraplane shot out of the cargo jet's underbelly! An instant later the wings of the craft swung outward from the fuselage.

As the wings bit into the air stream, Tom expected them to provide a smooth lifting effect. Instead, the ship gave a lurch that almost jarred the three occupants from their seats.

"R-r-ride 'em, cowboy!" Chow, white-faced, tried to force a grin as the small craft rocked and rolled alarmingly.

Tom fought the controls and managed to steady the ship. Then he steered it in a tight swooping circle to an altitude several hundred feet below the cargo jet.

"Now to try out the gas bag." Tom turned a valve on the control panel, feeding helium to the deflated dirigible bag.

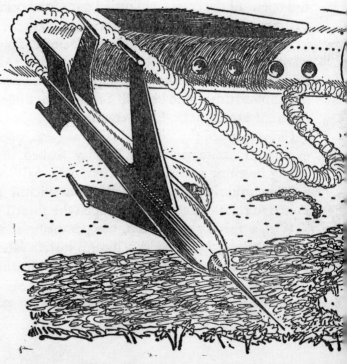

All three watched in awe through a transparent panel overhead as the bag slowly emerged from its pod. Bit by bit, it billowed out to full shape. Tom cut his jet power slowly as the bag took over the function of supporting the plane.

In little more than a minute, they were floating almost motionless above the jungle.

"Shucks, I knowed all the time it was goin' to work jest fine," Chow told his young boss.

"Wait till he starts letting the gas *out* of the bag," Bud teased. "We still have to get down, you know." Chow swallowed hard but said nothing.

The paraplane rocked and rolled alarmingly

The helium tanks were mounted in a small compartment at the rear of the cabin. Tom switched on an electric pump and compressor to suck the helium back into the tanks. A humming noise filled the cabin as the bag deflated. Gently the paraplane descended toward the treetops.

"I've got to hand it to you, genius boy." Bud slapped his chum on the back. "This new invention of yours may save a lot of lives some day."

"I hope so," Tom replied modestly. "In the meantime, let's also hope we don't get hung up in one of those trees down there."

Although Tom made no mention of it to Bud or Chow, a new worry came to mind. Despite all the preparations, how would these natives greet strangers who wanted to take away some of their citizens for scientific study? The medical college of Grandyke University, located near Shopton, the Swifts' home town, had made careful arrangements through the University of Mexico and the *aduana,* the combination immigration and customs department of the Mexican government for several healthy young Mayan men to be flown back to the States. But what if they were panicked into hostile action!

Still keeping his thoughts to himself, Tom steered the ship gently downward by means of the rudder and elevators. He aimed for a tiny open space in the forest. Presently a crowd of na-

tives came into view through the densely cluster-
ing green foliage.

"A reception committee!" Bud exclaimed.

"Reckon they look friendly enough," Chow
added, his Adam's apple bobbing up and down
nervously.

Tom smiled in relief as he saw the natives waving at them. He waved back and urged his two
companions to do likewise. The crowd gave way
good-naturedly as Tom set the paraplane down
in a gentle landing on the jungle floor.

When the three airmen emerged, they were
greeted by shouts of welcome. The Mayas surged
forward in friendly yet dignified fashion to inspect their visitors. Some offered large bouquets
of gorgeous-colored flowers.

"Sure are happy little critters!" Chow observed, grinning from ear to ear in relief.

The natives were handsome and brown-
skinned, with fine figures. But none were over
five feet tall, and many of them were considerably
shorter. The men were clad only in shorts, while
the women wore simple, straight white dresses,
with low square necklines embroidered in gay
colors and a matching trim on the skirts.

A swarm of naked little children hugged the
legs of their parents and peeped out bashfully at
the strangers from the sky. Many of the natives
chattered in a strange tongue.

"What kind o' lingo is that?" Chow asked.

"Old Mayan," Tom explained. "But some of the people also speak Spanish."

Before Tom could make a speech of reply to this friendly welcome, a stalwart old native raised his hand. Apparently he was chief of the village. At his signal, the crowd parted and a group of men dancers came forward.

All were adorned with tall headdresses of parrot feathers. While several other Indians beat tom-toms and blew on conch shells, the group began to perform a ceremonial dance.

"Brand my turkey giblets," Chow gasped, "they're actin' like birds!"

"I think that's what they're supposed to be imitating," Tom replied in a whisper.

The dancers gracefully hopped about, flapped their arms, and made pecking motions at each other.

Finally the performers finished and the three Americans applauded loudly. Then the chief stepped forward again.

Tom clasped his hand and spoke a few words to him in Spanish, which the chief understood. The young inventor then handed over several papers from the Mexican authorities, identifying the American visitors and stamped with an official seal.

As the chief read the papers, Bud whispered to

Tom, "He says he's the *ahau*, or king, no less, of these people!"

"And that his Spanish name is José," Tom added. "But we're to call him by his Mayan name —Quetzal."

"Quetzal?" Chow shoved back his ten-gallon hat and scratched his bald dome. "Ain't that a bird too?"

Tom nodded. "It's rare now, but the quetzal is a beautiful bird with brilliant long green plumage. It was sacred to ancient Mayas."

"They seem to be very fond of their feathered friends." Bud chuckled.

When Quetzal finished reading the papers, he handed them back to Tom. Then he beckoned forward five of the young Mayan men and introduced them by name to the Americans. All were very short in stature. "These are the ones who will accompany you," the chief said to Tom.

"My tribe and I desire that you stay at our village for the night," Quetzal went on. "We will have more entertainment for you."

Chow scowled suspiciously and murmured to Tom, "You figure that's safe?"

Tom grinned. "Still worried about those stewpots, Chow? I'm sure that we can trust these people."

Turning back to Quetzal, Tom accepted. He added that they must first notify the Americans who were hovering overhead in the cargo plane.

The chief nodded. "You come to the village when you are ready. My people and I will return there and make preparations." Then Quetzal turned and led his people away, down a narrow jungle path.

The three airmen re-entered their plane and Tom reported by radio to Slim Davis. "Find a landing spot for the night," he said. "I'll call you tomorrow morning when we're ready to be picked up."

"Roger!" Slim acknowledged.

Chow was still grumbling about staying overnight in this strange place as he climbed out of the paraplane with Tom and Bud. Suddenly the old Texan broke off with a gasp of fear and grabbed Tom by the arm.

"What's wrong now?" the young inventor asked.

"L-l-look!" Chow gulped, pointing with a trembling finger.

Tom heard a bloodcurdling snarl. Then, on the lowest branch of a nearby tree, he saw a ferocious-looking jaguar, its mouth open and its teeth bared.

The next moment a shot rang out!

CHAPTER II

THE SACRED STONE

AS THE sound of the shot died away, the jaguar leaped up the trunk of the tree and disappeared among the upper foliage.

"Quick! Into the plane!" Tom ordered. "That big cat might come back!"

"Who fired that shot?" Bud demanded. The husky, dark-haired young flier was still pale and shaken by their narrow escape.

"Just what I want to know," Tom said, peering out the window. "And was it meant for us, or for the jaguar?"

Bud straightened up with a fresh shock. "Hey! Are you implying that we have *human* enemies in this jungle?"

Tom shrugged thoughtfully. "Search me. That rifleshot was fired at close range, yet it missed the jaguar completely."

Bud and Chow exchanged worried glances.

Dangerous adventures were nothing new to Tom Swift Jr., as they both knew from experience. Soon after perfecting his first major invention, his Flying Lab, Tom had been forced to match wits with a deadly group of rebels in South America.

Other adventures had followed, not only underseas and at the South Pole, but even in outer space. In his latest exploit with his Space Solartron, the young inventor had rescued his father from Oriental kidnapers, while exploring the moon with his spaceship *Challenger*.

As Bud and Chow mulled over the situation, Tom decided to test the unknown rifleman's intentions. He opened the cabin door and fluttered a white handkerchief outside the plane.

The signal was greeted by a shrill laugh. A moment later a white man strode into view, carrying a high-powered rifle in his hands and a knapsack over one shoulder. He wore braided khaki breeches and embroidered shirt, and a pith helmet.

"Brand my armadillo soup, who's *this* critter?" Chow demanded. He stared at the newcomer in frank surprise.

"Let's find out," Tom replied.

The three Americans stepped from the plane to meet the stranger face to face. He was of medium height, slightly pudgy, and conveyed an air of careless elegance. Before speaking, he took out a silk handkerchief and dabbed his face delicately.

"You came along just in time." Tom smiled and held out his hand.

"Buenos días." The stranger shook Tom's hand with the tips of his fingers. His grin seemed slightly mocking.

"Are you a Mexican?" Bud asked. He was puzzled by the stranger's manner. Also, his brownish-blond hair and light complexion seemed unusual for a Latin-American.

"I was born in Boston," the man replied in a languid voice. "Actually, I consider myself neither an American nor a Mexican."

"Meaning what?" Bud asked bluntly.

"Let's say I prefer to call myself an internationalist." As Tom and Bud flashed each other quizzical glances, he went on suavely, "I'm down here studying archaeology and philology at the University of Mexico. My name is Wilson Hutchcraft."

Tom introduced himself and his two companions. Chow added suspiciously, "What're them two things you said you was studyin'?"

Hutchcraft laughed patronizingly at Chow's question. "Archaeology and philology. The first is the study of material remains of ancient cultures."

"Oh. You're one o' them fellers who dig up ole stones an' tombs an' suchlike?"

"You might put it that way. Philology, on the other hand, is the study of languages. I speak several, and just now I'm doing field work, learning various Indian dialects."

"Including Mayan?" Tom asked.

"Naturally," Hutchcraft replied. "You see, there are four branches of the Mayan tongue— Mam, Aguacateca, Chuje, and Jacalteca. But I'm very much interested in the local tribe because they use certain words and phrases which differ from any of those dialects."

Chow fanned himself with his ten-gallon hat and shook his head. "Sure sounds like gobbledy-gook to me."

"Anyhow," Tom said with a laugh, "it's lucky you happened along with a gun just now."

"If you're wise, you'll carry guns yourselves," Hutchcraft warned. "This jungle country can be dangerous."

Tom made no reply to this suggestion. Like his famous father, Tom Swift Sr., he felt that scientists should work for the peaceful advancement of mankind. In line with this belief, firearms were used only as a necessity on Swift expeditions.

Changing the subject, Tom explained the purpose of his flight to Yucatan. He invited Hutchcraft to join him and his friends in their visit to Quetzal's village.

"Delighted," the Bostonian replied. "As a matter of fact, I was on my way there just now."

With Tom in the lead, they started down the jungle trail toward the Mayan village. Twilight was falling over the steamy green rain forest, and the chattering birds began to hush. But the fading sunlight brought no cooling breeze to relieve the lowland heat. All four travelers were soon perspiring heavily as they tramped over the matted jungle path.

"The village is right ahead," Tom announced presently.

Quetzal's domain was little more than a huddle of palm-thatched huts. Cooking fires blazed in front of every dwelling. The women, crouched over open stone fireplaces, were patting tortilla cakes out of corn meal for the evening repast, while children played nearby and men chatted in groups.

As Ahau Quetzal came forward to greet the visitors, Tom said, "This is a new friend of ours, also a North American," and introduced Hutchcraft.

Quetzal invited the newcomer to stay, then took the visitors to a central fireplace, which Tom assumed served for village ceremonies and celebrations.

"I hope you will accept gifts of food from my people and that you will enjoy them," he said.

The gifts turned out to include a roasted wild turkey, a heaping supply of papaya fruit, guavas, bananas, and avocado pears, as well as several gourds full of coconut milk.

"Brand my lil ole cookstove, we got enough

grub here for a reg'lar feast!" Chow gloated.

The Americans ate with hungry zest. Even Hutchcraft, who had made several sneering comments about the primitive cooking conditions, admitted that the meal was very good.

By the time they finished, darkness had fallen. The sky over the jungle was brilliant with stars. "Sure is purty up there," Chow remarked, staring heavenward. "But it's even better back home in Texas," he added quickly.

Quetzal returned to make arrangements for the night. "You will sleep in my own house—the house of the ahau," he told them proudly.

Like the other dwellings in the village, the hut was made of saplings covered with mud. It was rectangular in shape, about twenty-five feet long, with walls ten feet high and a steep, palm-thatched roof. Although it had no windows, there was a doorway in the middle of each long side.

Hammocks woven of henequen fiber were slung in a row between the two doors. This, the chief explained, was to enable sleepers to catch the trade winds which occasionally wafted over the jungle. He also provided mosquito-netting covers for each hammock.

"I think I'd prefer sleeping out in the fresh air," Hutchcraft announced, sniffing the atmosphere of the hut disdainfully. He proceeded to unsling one of the hammocks.

"Reckon I'll do the same," Chow said.

But Hutchcraft's next remarks made Chow change his mind. "After all, I have a rifle and you don't," the Bostonian reminded him. "That jaguar might still be prowling around."

Soon the village was wrapped in silence. The three Americans in the hut quickly fell asleep. But suddenly Tom was awakened by a loud crash.

"Huh? Wh-what's going on?" Bud muttered thickly, trying to sit up in his hammock.

"Don't know yet," Tom replied tersely, fumbling in the darkness for his flashlight.

In a moment he extracted it from one pocket of his riding breeches, which he had hung on the wall nearby. As he switched on the beam, Bud came wide awake and gave a roar of laughter.

Chow, still half asleep, was sprawled on the floor of the hut, hopelessly tangled in his mosquito netting. He blinked and snorted in the dazzling yellow glow of the flashlight.

"What in thunderation happened?" the Texan grunted.

"Guess you fell out of your hammock," Tom replied, quaking with laughter. "Come on. I'll help you up."

Chow was hardly back in his swaying billet when loud snores announced that he was fast asleep again.

Tom chuckled. To Bud he whispered, "The fall didn't hurt him."

The next morning after breakfast Tom was

eager to be off. But again Quetzal delayed him.

"First we must have a leave-taking ceremony for the five men of my tribe who will go with you," the king explained.

The entire tribe gathered around the stone fireplace in the center of the village. All bowed their heads as a native priest blessed the five small men and offered prayers in Spanish.

Then a Maya, taller than the others, stepped forward. He wore metal arm bands, shell necklaces, a skirt made of jaguar skin, and a parrot-feather headdress.

"Now for the real ceremony. This fellow is a medicine man," Hutchcraft whispered contemptuously to the other Americans. "His tribe clings stubbornly to the pagan practices of its ancestors."

Several native bearers brought a large flat stone for the medicine man to stand on. He mounted it and began to utter an incantation in the old Mayan tongue.

Suddenly Tom's eyes bulged in surprise. The stone was carved in strange mathematical markings. They looked like the symbols used by the Swifts' mysterious friends in outer space to communicate with earth!

"Am I seeing things?" Tom wondered.

Groupings of similar mathematical symbols had been found on a polished black missile from outer space which had landed on the grounds of Swift Enterprises. Tom and his father had managed to decode the message and to reply by means of a powerful radio transmitter. Later, signals had been picked up with a special receiver using an oscilloscope-type screen.

Tom stepped forward to get a better look at the stone. The carvings on it were rather faint.

Suddenly a muscular native grabbed his arm and jerked him back. "Do not interrupt the sacred ceremony!" the man hissed in Spanish.

Tom waited tensely for the ceremony to end. He could hardly contain his curiosity as questions surged into his mind.

Was he mistaken about the carved symbols on the stone? Or were they really the same as those used in messages from his space friends? If so, how had they happened to appear in this remote jungle village?

"I must find out!" Tom determined. "I may have stumbled on a really big discovery!"

CHAPTER III

RELIC FROM SPACE

"WHAT'S wrong, pal?" Bud asked, noting Tom's puzzled frown.

"Take a look," Tom whispered, pointing to the stone on which the medicine man was standing. "Do those carvings strike you as familiar?"

Bud gasped in amazement. Chow was also dumfounded as his eyes followed Bud's glance. Both recognized the symbols immediately.

"Good night!" Bud muttered. "They look just like the stuff that comes through on the space oscilloscope!"

Tom nodded. "I certainly want to get a closer look."

As soon as the Mayan medicine man finished his incantation, the bearers lifted the stone to take it away. Tom touched Quetzal's arm.

"May I see the carvings on that stone?"

The ahau's eyes narrowed. He pondered a mo-

ment, then said, *"Muy bien."* He signaled the
bearers to bring the stone over to Tom, adding,
"But remember, *amigo,* you are gazing on our
most sacred possession."

Sacred! This made the find even more important, Tom thought.

He scrutinized the carvings. Some of the symbols were so weathered and faded that they could
hardly be seen. But Tom was able to decipher at
least part of the inscription. His heart beat with a
thrill of discovery!

Looking up at Quetzal, Tom pointed to one
row of symbols and translated: " 'Fifty of us flew
in here without mishap.' "

The effect on the chief was amazing. His mouth
dropped open and an expression of awe and fear
came into his eyes. Grabbing Tom by the arm,
Quetzal drew him aside from the crowd of natives.

"You are right!" he gasped. "But how did you
know? Can you read this writing carved by our
ancestors many hundreds of years ago?"

"Some, but not all of it," Tom replied. "You
see, I've received messages in such symbols myself—from people somewhere in the sky."

Using simple words, Tom told the chief about
the missile from outer space which had landed at
Swift Enterprises. He also tried to explain about
later communications received, which both he
and his father were certain came from the inhab-
itants of space, possibly the planet Mars.

Chief Quetzal's eyes grew wider and wider as he listened, even though it was clear that he failed to understand all of what Tom was saying.

"This must mean that some of our ancestors came from the sky!" Quetzal exclaimed proudly. "This stone has always belonged to my people. Unfortunately," he added sadly, "I know the meaning of only one other part of the inscription."

Pointing to another group of symbols on the stone, Quetzal translated: " 'We will hunt for the rest of the armada.' "

"An armada of spaceships from another planet!" Tom thought to himself excitedly.

A fleet manned by space beings must have landed in the jungle centuries ago! Was it possible that these space people were similar to humans, had intermarried with people who had lived here originally, and were the ancestors of this particular tribe?

Tom asked the king if he could tell him any legends about his ancestors coming to Yucatan. But Quetzal shook his head.

"One thing I do not understand," he said. "Why did my people long ago write with these strange signs? They are not like the picture writing the rest of the old Mayas used."

"The space people know that mathematics are the only *exact* 'language'—a language which never changes," Tom answered. "I believe they wrote in these symbols, so that people from any planet at any time could read and translate the message, even though they did not speak any earth language."

The chief sighed and looked at Tom with great respect. "You are no doubt right, amigo." It was plain that he was very much impressed by the young inventor's knowledge.

Tom's brain was seething with excitement. What had happened to the space voyagers? Had part of the armada been wrecked during the jungle landing? Maybe traces of their space craft could still be found!

Aloud, he said to Quetzal, "Perhaps your ancestors left other carved stones or relics. May we search the forest?"

The chief shrugged. "The government of Mexico has laws about such things. You must get their permission to do any digging."

"I'll certainly do that!" Tom promised. "Then I'll be back."

Meanwhile, Hutchcraft had been watching the speakers from a distance with great curiosity. He plied Bud and Chow with questions, trying to find out the reasons for Tom's interest in the sacred stone. Both dodged his queries, thinking it wiser not to reveal any information of importance without Tom's permission.

"Guess it's time we started back to the plane," Tom said when he finally rejoined them.

"Fine. But what happened to our passengers?" Bud added, looking around.

The five Mayas who were to accompany them to Shopton had disappeared! Alarmed, Tom asked Chief Quetzal where they had gone.

"Have no fear," the ahau replied. "They are merely preparing for the journey." With a proud gesture, he indicated the group, just emerging from a nearby hut.

There was no doubt but that they were the five volunteers. But in place of their usual white cotton shorts, the small natives were now wearing ill-fitting city business suits!

One of the suits was bright blue serge, one was brown tweed, and the other three loud checkered patterns. All the clothes were so large for their wearers that the sleeves and trouser cuffs had been rolled back. Each man wore a felt hat pulled down over his ears.

Tom, Bud, and Chow almost broke into laughter, but managed to stifle their mirth. Hutchcraft giggled shrilly until Tom silenced him with a warning glance. The five little Mayas were obviously bursting with pride at their "civilized" apparel.

Tom complimented the Indians on their fine appearance, and asked the chief where the clothes had come from.

"We sent a runner to the city of Mérida to order them," Quetzal explained.

The natives were wearing ill-fitting business suits

"Wal, I'll be a horned toad!" Chow chuckled under his breath.

The group set out from the Mayan village. Nearly the whole tribe tagged along. Hutchcraft, however, remained behind, saying he saw no reason to waste his energy unnecessarily.

When they reached the paraplane, Tom thanked Ahau Quetzal and his people for their hospitality. Then the travelers climbed aboard.

Tom took his place at the controls and made radio contact with the cargo jet. "We're ready to take off," he informed Slim Davis.

"Be right with you, skipper!" Slim replied.

Turning the release valve, Tom waited for the helium bag to inflate. But nothing happened!

"What's wrong?" Bud asked.

"Don't know," Tom replied in a puzzled voice. "I'd better check the tanks." A moment later, after inspecting the pressure gauges, he turned a grave face to his companions.

"The tanks are empty!" Tom reported.

CHAPTER IV

A HELIUM MYSTERY

BUD sprang out of his seat and hurried aft to join the young inventor. "You mean the liquid helium leaked out?" he asked in alarm.

"It leaked out, all right," Tom replied grimly. "The loading cock is wide open."

"Good grief! How did that happen?"

Tom gave a worried shrug. "Maybe I got careless and opened it accidentally. But frankly, I don't even remember touching the tanks before we left the ship. How about you two?"

Both Bud and Chow denied knowing anything about it. Chow, who was dripping with sweat and fanning himself as usual with his sombrero, added, "Mebbe it's this broilin' hot weather. Must've made the helium swell up an' bust out."

Tom shook his head. "The helium wouldn't expand enough to force the loading cock!" He wondered uneasily if someone might have tampered with the plane during their absence. "We'd better check out the whole ship to make sure nothing else is wrong," he decided.

With Bud's help, Tom hastily checked the jet engines, landing gear, instruments, and other parts. But the paraplane showed no other sign of sabotage.

"Okay. Now what?" Bud asked.

"Looks as if we'll have to hike out of this jungle on foot," Tom replied.

"What about the plane? You're not going to abandon it here, are you?"

Tom hesitated, turning the matter over rapidly in his mind. "Look," he said to Bud and Chow, "would you two mind staying here a while to guard it?"

Both agreed. "What about you, Tom?" Chow queried.

"I'll take the five Mayas and trek to the nearest spot where Slim can land," Tom explained. "Then I'll call Shopton and ask Dad to send us everything we need, including more helium." In a low voice he added, "Now that I've seen the sacred stone, I'd like to stay down here to do some digging, and let Slim take the Mayas to Shopton."

During the trek to the plane from the Mayan village, Tom had told his two companions the brief translation from the stone. He had also mentioned his hope of finding other stones—or perhaps even wreckage from the space armada.

"Suits me," Bud nodded. Chow also agreed, although without much enthusiasm for a prolonged stay in the hot Yucatan jungle.

Meanwhile, the horde of natives clustered around curiously, baffled by the delay in take-off. Tom explained his plight to Chief Quetzal, and asked for native guides to accompany him on a trek to the nearest spot where the cargo jet could land.

"*Si*," the king assured him. "We are glad to help our white friends any way we can."

Suddenly shouts arose from several of the keen-eyed Indians.

"It's Slim!" Bud exclaimed eagerly.

Looking skyward, Tom saw the cargo jet just winging into view. Climbing back aboard the paraplane, he made radio contact with the other ship.

"How come you're not upstairs?" Slim asked. "Anything wrong?"

Tom reported the mysterious loss of helium from the plane's tanks. "We'll have to leave the ship here for the time being," he concluded. "Where can you set down?"

"About ten miles from here," Slim replied.

"Can you give me a bearing?"

"Sure." There was a pause as Slim checked his compass, then his voice came back over the radio. "Bearing approximately one-seven-three degrees, skipper."

"Okay. Now listen," Tom said briskly. "Make up a bundle of hiking clothes, machetes, canteens of fresh water, and a hand compass—everything we'll need and let it down to us here. You'll find the stuff stowed in the cargo hold in a crate marked 'Emergency.' Then land and wait for us."

"Roger!"

Within a few minutes, the cargo jet hovered down close to the treetops. The loading hatch opened and a cable was payed out with the bundled-up jungle gear hooked to its lower end.

Tom and Bud quickly removed the bundle and the cable was reeled back into the plane. Dipping its wings in a farewell salute, the cargo jet soared off to the south.

"There's gear for you fellows here, too," Tom told Bud and Chow as he unpacked the bundle. "May as well wear this stuff—it'll be more comfortable and safer in the jungle."

The three Americans quickly changed clothes inside the ship. When they emerged, all were wearing khaki shirts and riding breeches tucked into high-laced boots. Tom and Bud wore sun helmets. But Chow, as usual, preferred his ten-gallon hat.

"I'm ready to leave," Tom told Chief Quetzal in Spanish.

"*Vaya con Dios*. Go with God," the ahau replied, shaking hands gravely. He signaled to the "medical" quintet, who had stripped off their store clothes and bundled them on their backs. The chief next beckoned to two natives he had selected to accompany Tom to the ship and bring him back.

"Good luck, pal," said Bud.

"Thanks. Take it easy, you two. I'll return as soon as possible."

Armed with compass, canteen, and machete, Tom plunged off into the jungle in a southerly direction with his seven Mayan companions. The natives had long hooked knives, as well as water gourds and two rifles between them. They swung the knives with easy, freehand strokes to cut away any vines or underbrush that barred the way. This was done so smoothly and rapidly that the Indians almost seemed to glide through the dense jungle.

Tom found it hard to keep up with them. Jogging along at a fast trot, he was soon perspiring profusely and would have doffed his shirt except for the stinging insects that buzzed around him constantly.

"Boy, I should've practiced up for this jungle bit," Tom thought with a rueful grin.

It was late afternoon when he and the Mayas finally reached the cargo jet. The ship had landed in a sizable clearing.

"Hi, skipper!" Slim and the other crewmen greeted Tom with backslaps and good-natured ribbing about the stranded paraplane.

"Fine place you picked to run out of gas!" joked Arv Hanson. He was a husky six-footer, who built the precision scale models for all Tom's major inventions.

"All I can say is, it's a good thing all of us don't have to walk home," Tom replied with a chuckle.

The seven natives were overcome with awe at sight of the huge jet plane. In their halting Spanish, they plied Tom with questions and compliments about the "big bird from sky."

"They sure are pint-sized," Slim remarked as he watched the natives inspect the ship from all sides with excited-sounding comments in Mayan.

"True." Tom nodded. "But good friends to have in country like this."

Climbing aboard the plane, he soon made radio contact with the plant in Shopton. George Dilling, the Enterprises radio chief, summoned Tom's father, who spoke over a microphone in his office in the main building.

"How are things going, son?" the famous scientist asked. "Did you pick up the Mayas for the medical research project at Grandyke?"

"Yes, Dad, but Slim will bring them. I can't come back right away." Tom related the misfortune that had left the paraplane grounded. "We'll need new tanks of helium. But there's something more important than that. I've made a terrific discovery!"

Breathlessly Tom described the sacred stone

with its symbols which told of a landing by a space armada.

Mr. Swift was amazed. "Tom, this may be far more important than the medical project!" he exclaimed. "A landing here on earth by space creatures centuries ago! Why, it staggers the imagination!"

"It sure does," Tom agreed. "Another thing, Dad. If that first space fleet met with disaster, it may explain why our present space friends feel they don't understand our atmosphere and are afraid to try entering it."

"You're right, son. We must find out all we can and send a full report on the symbols' significance to our space friends," Mr. Swift went on. "Can you translate any more from the stone if I send a copy of our space dictionary?"

This codebook, which the two Swifts had compiled, contained all the mathematical symbols translated from earlier messages.

"I'm afraid the carving is too worn and faint," Tom explained. "That's why I want you to send the pilot model of the new camera I've been working on."

"Your electronic retroscope?"

"Right, Dad. I'm sure it can help us decipher the rest of the carving."

Tom's latest invention was designed to "see" what a rock face—or any other surface—looked like originally, before being exposed to wear or erosion. Tom believed that it would prove highly useful in scientific research by geologists, archaeologists, and paleontologists.

The camera was based on two earlier achievements of the Swifts. One was Tom's discovery of a hitherto unknown electromagnetic radiation given off by all matter. This had led to the invention of the Swift spectroscope and the force-ray repelatron used in Tom's latest spaceship.

The new camera also made use of certain detector features invented by Mr. Swift and used in Tom's "Eye-Spy" camera which could take motion pictures through a wall or other solid object.

"If my retroscope works," Tom went on, "it'll not only show us the original carving, but help us determine the date of the space armada's landing. I'm hoping we can find some other carved stones or perhaps traces of wreckage of the space vehicles. But we'll need permission from the Mexican government to dig."

"I'll arrange that through our State Department," Mr. Swift promised.

"Fine. I'd like you to send the Flying Lab down here, Dad. And besides the camera and helium, please ship along a jeep, a small tank, and all the digging equipment we'll need."

Mr. Swift agreed to attend to these details. He also assured Tom that he would be on hand to greet the shy little Mayan men when they arrived in Shopton and escort them personally to Grandyke University. "Take care of yourself, son," the elder scientist concluded.

"I will, Dad. And give my love to Mother and Sis."

By the time Tom had signed off, the sky had darkened considerably. He emerged from the cargo ship to find a stiff wind blowing in from the sea. The Mayas stood huddled together rather fearfully. They greeted Tom with chattering exclamations in broken Spanish.

"What're they saying, skipper?" Slim asked.

"That we're in for a storm," Tom replied. "We'd better all hop aboard and make sure everything's secure."

He and Slim went at once to the pilot's and copilot's seats. Presently Tom checked with the crew who had gone aft. All doors were locked.

By this time the storm had broken. A torrential rain poured down on the jungle, making visibility almost zero. The wind increased to gale force.

Watching through the pilot's window, the boys saw the nearby trees bend under the smashing impact of the wind. Suddenly the plane itself began to shudder and move.

"We're being pushed backward by the wind!" Slim cried. "Tom, we'll crash into the trees!"

CHAPTER V

A DISMAYING FAILURE

INSTANTLY Tom's hands flew to the controls and he gunned the jet engines into life.

"Going to try for a take-off?" Slim shouted as the plane lurched and swayed.

"Too dangerous in this storm," Tom replied tersely. "But maybe I can hold us off from crashing into the forest!" He opened the throttle slowly and fed the forward jets enough power for ordinary taxiing.

Gradually Tom was able to adjust the jet blast to a force just great enough to counteract the wind pressure. The whole plane vibrated under the terrible stress. But at last it halted its dangerous backward motion. The ship's tail assembly was scarcely a yard short of the nearest belt of trees!

"Whew!" Slim mopped his forehead. "That's what I call too close for comfort!"

The roar of the hurricane winds outside and the clattering impact of the rain against the plane's fuselage made it almost impossible for Tom and Slim to hear each other's voices.

"I'll see how the rest are making out," Tom said finally. "Take over, pal."

Leaving the flight cabin, he went aft through a narrow passageway. In the crew's compartment, he found Bob Jeffers and Bill Bennings. But there were no jungle passengers.

"Hey, where are the Mayas?" Tom asked.

The crewmen looked at each other blankly. Then Bob Jeffers spoke up. "Gosh, skipper, we thought they were with you!"

Tom turned pale. Had the Mayas changed their minds and run away? Tom groaned. He had assumed the task of bringing the little men to Grandyke University and now he had failed!

"It's my fault," he assured the worried crewmen. "I should have made certain the Mayas came aboard."

The trio rushed to the plane's windows to peer outside. The streaming moisture on the heavy panes and the sheets of water falling made it hard for them to see outside. But no Mayas were in sight.

"Maybe they didn't run away for good," Bob suggested. "They may have figured this plane wouldn't be safe in the storm."

Tom was not convinced. Still worried, he

opened the door of the compartment and poked his head out into the rain for a better view. The crewmen heard him gasp.

"See something, skipper?" Bill Bennings asked.

"Those store clothes the Mayas were carrying all bundled up on their backs—they've dumped them on the ground at the edge of the clearing!"

"Probably too heavy to bother with, once they got soaked."

"That's just it," Tom agreed. "Why leave them to get soaked? If those men ducked for shelter, why didn't they take the clothes with them? They were mighty proud of those suits."

"It does look as if they've run out on us," Bob agreed, "but they may not be far away. Let's look for them as soon as the rain stops."

The storm ended as abruptly as it had begun. Tom and Bob hurried outside and the young inventor shouted in Spanish for the Mayas to return. There was no answer.

"Now what?" Bob asked.

"We'll just have to go after them. Surely they'd head for the village."

He and Bob followed the cleared trail through the forest and were able to travel at a good pace despite the soggy earth. Within ten minutes they caught sight of the native volunteers and their companions. The men were huddled in the middle of the jungle path chattering intently.

The Mayas broke off at Tom's approach and stared at him rather apprehensively out of their almost jet-black eyes. Tom greeted them:

"*Qué tienen, amigos?* Are you five not going to the *Estados Unidos* as you promised? Surely a Maya does not break his word!"

The volunteers looked at one another uncomfortably. Being courteous and trustworthy by nature, they seemed embarrassed at Tom's words.

"We do not wish to break our promise," one stammered in his broken Spanish. "But we are afraid. That storm was a bad omen."

Tom's brain worked swiftly to find a suitable answer. "As you see, the storm has caused no harm," he pointed out. "Perhaps your ancestors in the sky were merely weeping at your departure. But you will return to Yucatan later."

"Sí, that is so," the Mayan spokesman said, brightening.

After conversing together for a few moments, the volunteers finally agreed to return with Tom to the plane. Tom told the two guides that his father was sending down a car by plane, and therefore he would not need their services for the return trip. He thanked them and they started back to the village.

Arv Hanson and the crewmen greeted Tom with grins of relief when his party arrived at the cargo ship. Arv, a first-rate amateur chef, was already preparing the evening meal in the plane's galley. The Mayas sampled the food a bit suspiciously, but soon broke into broad smiles of enjoyment and wolfed down every morsel.

"Even *they* like your Swedish *smörgåsbord*, Arv!" Slim said with a chuckle.

Early the next morning the *Sky Queen* came streaking into view over the jungle. The huge, atomic-powered three-decker plane—Tom's first major invention—came down with pinpoint precision on its jet lifters, in the clearing beside the cargo ship.

Tom had nicknamed his mighty craft the Flying Lab because it was completely equipped for scientific research in any part of the globe.

"Hi, skipper!" Doc Simpson, the young Enterprises medic, was first to climb down from the plane. He greeted Tom with a bear hug.

"Good to see you, Doc," Tom replied with a grin. "Same goes for you, Dick and Jack."

His latter remark was directed to Jack Murray and Dick Folsom, two of Swift Enterprises' brilliant young engineering staff.

"We decided to come along and see how your new camera works," Jack explained, as they all shook hands.

"Good deal. Any message from Dad?"

"I brought a letter," Doc replied, taking it from a pocket and handing it over.

Tom read the letter eagerly. Mr. Swift had written that the Mexican government would permit digging only if supervised by an expert from the Institute of Anthropology and History of Yucatan. They promised to send a man named Señor Marco Barancos to meet the Flying Lab.

"Just as well," Tom thought. "He can probably give us some valuable help."

Doc Simpson was eager to examine the Mayas. He told Tom that their basal metabolism—the rate at which their bodies used energy—was five to eight per cent higher than that of the average North American.

Tom introduced Doc to the five young natives, who seemed immensely pleased by his interest and attention. They accompanied him willingly into the sick-bay compartment of the Flying Lab. Tom followed.

First Doc examined the Mayas' fine white teeth and exclaimed admiringly when he found no sign of dental decay.

"That will be a good subject for the Grandyke study," he said. "It may have something to do with their diet. Here's another interesting feature," he added, as he examined their eyes. "Notice this trace of a fold of flesh at the inner corner of each eye, called the epicanthic fold. When large, it's what gives Orientals their slant-eyed appearance."

"That seems to bear out the theory that Indian tribes either crossed over to this continent from Asia and settled here, or started here and went the other way," Tom commented.

As Doc proceeded to give the Mayas a more detailed examination, Tom left the sick bay and hurried up to his private laboratory. Dick Folsom and Jack Murray went with him, eager to learn more about his electronic retroscope.

"We looked the equipment over on our flight down here," Dick said, "but frankly we don't understand how it works."

The setup was in three parts. The camera itself consisted of several electronic devices, connected by cable to two large console units, each one studded with dials and controls.

"It looks complicated, but the basic principle is fairly simple," Tom said. "As you know, any rock may undergo radioactive aging as its natural elements break down and become other elements. That happens all through the rock. But the layers nearer the surface are more exposed to cosmic radiation from the outside."

"Your dad said that you're interested in studying some rock carvings," put in Jack. "A carved surface means that different layers of rock are exposed all at one time."

"Exactly," said Tom. "For instance, if you carve a gouge in the rock, the cosmic radiation would penetrate deeper at that point than it would in an uncarved part of the rock. Therefore, the radioactivity *inside* the rock follows the same in-and-out depth pattern as the carving on the rock's surface."

"Wait a minute!" Dick snapped his fingers. "I think I get it. By measuring the radioactivity all through the rock, you can figure out what the carving looked like before it was worn away!"

"Right," Tom said. "Now, my camera here has two detectors. One scans the whole surface of the rock to probe out differences in radioactivity; the other stays focused on one unworn spot on the rock surface to show the basic level of the rock's radioactive aging."

Jack pointed to the first of the two large console units. "I suppose this electronic brain takes the information from your detectors and calculates how much of the rock has been worn away at every point."

Tom nodded. "And this master time dial here shows the age of the rock since the carving was made. The computer uses this reading for comparison with the slight changes in radioactivity as indicated by the scanner."

Dick asked about the purpose of the console unit which had a cathode-ray screen.

"That's the reproducing unit," Tom explained. "The brain's output is fed into a cathode-ray tube, so as to give us a picture of what the original rock surface looked like—just as on a TV screen. The output is also fed into this lower part of the unit, where the picture is reproduced on photographic film as a permanent record."

The expressions on the two engineers' faces showed their intense admiration of Tom's newest invention.

"Quite a gadget!" Dick said, slapping Tom on the back. "How soon can we give it a tryout?"

"Right now, if we can find any old Mayan stone carvings around here."

By the time they emerged from Tom's laboratory, the cargo jet was ready to take off on its return flight to Shopton. Tom shook hands with the

The iguana reared up on its hind legs and lunged at Tom

five Mayas and reassured them with a few parting words in Spanish. Then they climbed aboard, where Slim, Arv, and the other crewmen helped to make them comfortable. A few moments later the plane rose smoothly.

Tom, Doc, and the two engineers now fanned out to search for marked stones. "Better not stray too far from the clearing," Tom warned.

Minutes later, he yelled, "Think I've found one!" and the others hurried to join him. Tom pointed to a round, weather-beaten stone lying almost hidden in the tall grass. It bore faint carvings.

"Let's see if we can lift it," Tom said, bending down to pry the stone loose.

The next instant he recoiled with a startled gasp. A green iguana, almost six feet long from tip to tail, had suddenly raised its ugly head from the undergrowth! Rearing up on its hind legs with jaws open, the reptile lunged as if to rake Tom's face with its claws.

"Good grief!" Tom gulped, jumping back hastily in the nick of time.

"You really scared that poor lizard, Tom," Doc Simpson teased. "That's why she went for you. Iguanas really aren't as fierce as they look."

"Just the same, I won't try taking this one for a pet," Tom said with a rueful chuckle.

After a brief search, another carved stone was found. The group carried it back to the Flying Lab.

Tom quickly set up his camera, flicked a switch, and began tuning several dials. "These markings look fairly recent—not more than a thousand years old," he remarked jokingly, "but it's good enough for a test."

The others watched the cathode-ray screen

with intense interest. But the resulting picture was a mere blur! Tom made numerous adjustments without success. His face filled with dismay.

Was his new invention a failure?

CHAPTER VI

THE GIANT FIGURE

"ANY idea what's wrong?" Dick Folsom asked.

"Not yet." The young inventor unscrewed the rear panel of the camera's reproducing unit. "Have to check a few of these circuits first."

Doc and the two engineers watched as he probed deftly among the maze of electronic parts. Using an oscilloscope and several other testing devices, Tom made a quick check of the reproducer, then the "brain," and finally each part of the scanning apparatus.

"What's the verdict, trouble shooter?" Jack Murray asked, as the young scientist finished examining the setup.

"Everything checks out," Tom said gloomily, "so the fault must be in my design. I have a hunch it's the scanner. Apparently it doesn't 'see' the stone in enough detail for the reproducer to form a clear picture."

"Boy, you've got a job on your hands, skipper."

Dick frowned as he examined the two detectors with a professional eye. "My guess is that redesigning your camera 'eyes' will take at least a week's work back at the plant."

"Can't wait that long—I need the retroscope now while we're here in Yucatan." Tom ran his fingers through his crewcut. "Maybe I'm taking a long shot, but I'm going to try turning out a new rig right here in the Flying Lab."

"A tall order, Tom!" Jack Murray whistled. "But you can do it if anyone can."

Bob and Doc nodded vigorously, and Bob said, "We'd better clear out, so you can work undisturbed."

The door had hardly closed behind the three when Tom plunged into his problem. He whipped out a slide rule and began making rapid calculations.

"One thing's certain," Tom thought. "To get finer detail in the picture, and still keep the rig down to portable size, I'll have to miniaturize the whole scanning apparatus. And that brings up another problem—stepping up the mechanical operation of the scanner, too, so it'll work at faster speed. Hmm . . ."

Hours went by. Tom's desk became littered with scribbled equations, circuit diagrams, and sketches of part layouts. Finally he broke off long enough to buzz the galley over the intercom and ask for food.

Minutes later, a crewman brought a tray of hot soup and sandwiches up to his lab. "Still at it, skipper?"

Tom nodded as he began munching on a roast-beef sandwich. He was deep in his calculations again before the crewman had even closed the laboratory door.

By nightfall Tom had begun to rig up a new miniaturized scanner, even though he was still not certain he had licked the problem completely. Some time later he glanced at his wrist watch.

"Ten after twelve." The young inventor gave a whistle. "What a skullcracker this turned out to be! Dick sure wasn't kidding when he guessed it would take a week's work."

Leaning back on his laboratory stool, Tom stretched his cramped limbs. "Sure wish Bud and Chow were here," he thought wistfully. Bud's breezy quips and Chow's many puzzled questions not only gave Tom a lift, but often played a part in giving him a new insight into whatever problem he was tackling.

Soon he was back at work assembling a mass of tiny spiderlike transistors, diodes, and other semiconductors. But presently Tom's head slumped toward the workbench and he drowsed off from sheer exhaustion.

Meanwhile, Bud Barclay and Chow were turning and tossing in their hammocks, back in the

Mayan village. A horde of tiny insects buzzed maddeningly outside their mosquito netting.

Presently Bud whispered, "Hey, Chow! You awake?"

"I sure am," the cook grunted. "These pesky flyin' buzzsaws are drivin' me plumb loco, let alone all them jungle noises out there!"

"You suppose the paraplane's safe?"

Chow raised up on one shoulder. The moonlight shining in through the door of the hut showed a worried look on his weather-beaten face. "It better be if we're ever aimin' to get out o' this jungle. Why? You figger it ain't?"

"I don't know what to figure," Bud replied restlessly.

"Tom told us to come back here to the village at night," Chow pointed out. "We sure couldn't bunk down out in the jungle with them jaguars an' all without even a six-shooter between us!"

"I know, but even so . . ." Bud hesitated. "Suppose Tom's hunch was right, and someone did try to sabotage the plane by opening the helium cocks. How do we know he won't come back tonight and pull another trick?"

Chow exclaimed in alarm. "Brand my britches, now you got *me* worried! Come on, Buddy boy. You an' me better hop out there an' take a look-see—jest to make sure!"

Pulling on their clothes, the pair tiptoed out

of the hut and made their way through the sleeping village. As they passed the outer fringe, just beyond the native huts, Bud suddenly grabbed Chow's arm. He pointed to an empty hammock slung between two trees.

"Hey, look!" Bud hissed. "Hutchcraft's not in his bed!"

Chow paused, shoved back his cowboy hat, and scratched his bald head. "Where d'you s'pose Mr. Fancy Pants has gone to? I never did trust that hombre!"

"Same here," Bud muttered. "Oh, well, no use wasting time on him. Come on! We've got to make sure the paraplane's okay."

Luckily a full moon was riding high over the treetops. Otherwise it would have been impossible for the two Americans to pick their way along the jungle trail in the darkness.

As they neared the ship, Chow gave a hoarse croak and froze in his tracks. "B-B-Bud!" he gasped. "Do you see what I see?"

"I sure do!"

The two could hardly believe their eyes. A huge hulking figure, which looked at least seven feet tall, was moving furtively near the nose of the paraplane! Suddenly the figure darted off with surprising quickness into the leafy underbrush.

"What in tarnation was it?" Chow gulped. "A gorilla?"

"Not around here!" Gathering his wits, Bud

spurted forward. "Come on! Let's see where it went! I want a closer look!"

Together, they reached the plane and plunged into the underbrush where the giant form had disappeared.

"Leapin' rattlesnakes!" Chow quavered, as they groped about among the tangled creepers and head-high jungle growth. "It's so dark in here I can't tell which is you an' which is me!"

His nervous wisecrack seemed hardly an exaggeration. Scarcely a ray of moonlight pierced the darkness, now that they had left the beaten trail.

"Guess you're right," Bud agreed. "We don't stand much chance of finding him—or it—now."

Giving up the search, they made a quick check of the paraplane. Everything seemed to be in order.

"What do we do now, pardner?" Chow asked.

Bud shrugged helplessly. "Not much we *can* do, I guess, except go back to the village. Whatever that was we saw, I have a hunch it won't risk a return visit—not tonight, anyhow."

"An' if it does, I'd jest as soon not have to fight it!" Chow confessed.

"You and me both." Bud chuckled ruefully. "Well, I guess we scared him away. Just the same, Chow, I believe we've picked up a clue to the mystery of who tampered with our helium tanks."

Still discussing the giant figure, the two tramped back through the jungle. When they reached the village, they were surprised to find Hutchcraft in his hammock, sound asleep.

"Wal, I'll be a bobtailed bronc!" Chow exclaimed. "Wonder where he went?"

"I intend to find out," Bud vowed grimly.

The next morning, when they gathered for breakfast, Bud asked the Bostonian about his mysterious absence during the night.

"I went to get some insect repellent out of my gear," Hutchcraft replied calmly. "I have it stowed in the village. For that matter," he added, "what were you two doing up wandering around?"

Bud told of their visit to the plane and the hulking figure they had sighted. Hutchcraft could throw no light on the mystery. "Sounds to me as if you both were having a nightmare," he remarked with a needling chuckle.

Chow snorted angrily, but said nothing. After breakfast Bud described the intruder to Ahau Quetzal. The chief stared fearfully at the two Americans.

After a long pause, he replied, "Maybe it was the cave man—the giant who can crush a jaguar with his bare hands!"

CHAPTER VII

MIGHTY MAX

BUD and Chow looked at each other in astonishment. A giant in the Yucatan jungle? A cave man powerful enough to kill jaguars with his bare hands! It sounded weird! Yet there was certainly *some* kind of giant lurking out in the bush—they had seen him with their own eyes!

"Brand my griddlecakes, it don't make sense!" Chow muttered.

"Have you seen the giant yourself?" Bud asked Quetzal in halting Spanish. He had learned to speak a little of the language during Tom's Flying Lab adventure in South America. Chow, too, had picked up some pidgin Spanish in his Texas days. "Tell us more, please," Bud urged the chief. "Who is this giant? Where did he come from?"

Quetzal looked at the two white men as if he failed to understand. When Bud repeated his questions, the chief shrugged and mumbled something in the Mayan tongue.

"Reckon he jest don't *want* to understand," Chow whispered.

"Guess you're right," Bud agreed under his breath. "I'd better change the subject."

The chief's unblinking stare made both Americans feel somewhat uncomfortable. However, he seemed as friendly as ever when Bud spoke of other things, such as Tom's return to dig for more relics.

"Your friend is a very wise young man," Quetzal said approvingly. "Perhaps he will find another stone carved by my people's ancestors."

As the chief walked away, Bud turned to Chow with a puzzled frown. "What do you make of it?"

Chow shrugged. "Must be mighty skeered o' that there giant. So skeered he don't even want to talk about it."

"I mean, what do you make of that stuff he told us—the cave-man business, and crushing jaguars?"

"It beats me," the Texan replied with a chuckle. "I sure ain't hankerin' to buddy up with the critter! An' if you're askin' me what an over-size cave man's doin' in this pygmy country, I can't make head nor tail o' that."

"Neither can I," Bud confessed. "Another thing. If that's the guy who sabotaged our helium tanks, what's his game?"

Chow shook his head. "I reckon there's no tellin' what a loco jungle critter might do."

Bud nodded thoughtfully. "Maybe he's just

curious about the plane. Speaking of that, we'd better go back and stand guard."

Leaving the village, the two set off down the jungle path again. When they reached the para-plane, Bud made another quick check of the craft, both inside and out.

"Everything hunky-dory?" Chow asked.

"Seems to be. Let's call Tom and make a report." After warming up the set, Bud spoke into the microphone. "Barclay calling Swift jet! Come in, please!"

To his surprise, it was the Flying Lab which answered. "Hey! When did you fellows arrive?" Bud asked the radioman.

"Yesterday, but the skipper stuck around to tinker with his new camera. Wouldn't work right when he tried it out," the radioman explained. "Wait a sec. I'll get him on the intercom."

A moment later Tom's voice came over the air. "Hi, pal! What cooks?"

"You won't believe me when I tell you," Bud replied. Quickly Bud related how he and Chow had sighted a giant lurking near the plane the night before.

"A *giant!*" Tom gasped, then broke into a wry chuckle. "Are you sure you two weren't seeing things?"

"I said you wouldn't believe me," Bud retorted. "But it's no joke. Quetzal knows all about him— or *it*—or whatever you want to call the thing.

Claims he's some kind of cave man who kills jaguars with his bare hands!"

Bud went on to describe the chief's fearful reaction and his evasive manner when questioned further about the huge creature.

"The whole thing sounds crazy," Tom said in a mystified voice. "But you're right—this may explain how our helium supply was sabotaged." The young inventor was silent for a moment, then added, "Better stay there at the plane till I arrive. I'll start right away."

"Okay. And say, genius boy," Bud put in before Tom signed off, "Mac tells me your new camera didn't pan out so well. Won't you be able to use it on any space carvings we find down here?"

"We'll use it," Tom assured him. "In fact, that's exactly what I've been doing." He reported enthusiastically that after working half the night and resuming at dawn, he had succeeded in redesigning the scanner. Just before Bud's radio call, he had tested the camera again.

"I tried it out on an old Mayan inscribed stone we found near here," Tom went on. "The retroscope showed clearly what the original carving looked like. Turned out that it was four baktuns old."

Bud's brow puckered into a frown. "Four which?"

"Four baktuns." Tom chuckled. "Dad sent down some books on Mayan culture, and I've been reading up on their calendar and system of numbers. A baktun is four hundred years. The actual date as it appears on the stone is *8.14.0.0.0 7 Ahau 3 Xul,* which would be September first, A.D. 317, by our calendar."

"Wow! Over sixteen hundred years old!" Bud gave a whistle. "That's plenty ancient for me! But how do you know that date is accurate?"

"Because it checked out exactly with the reading on the time dial of my retroscope," Tom explained. "Besides, the old Mayas just didn't make mistakes when it came to dates. By means of astronomy they were able to figure out the length of a solar year right on the button. And they were wizards with numbers."

Tom went on to explain how the Mayas had developed two kinds of numerical notations. One, using a system of bars and dots, was simpler and easier to figure out than Roman numerals. The other, using pictures of human heads to represent the numbers from one to thirteen and also zero, was much like our present-day Arabic numerals.

"What's even more amazing," Tom told Bud, "the old Mayas were first to develop an accurate calendar and to reckon time from a fixed date. They were able to figure out the length of a year so closely that their calendar was actually more accurate than the one Americans were using at the time George Washington was born."

"Must've been smart cookies," Bud said, impressed. "It's strange how such a great civilization as theirs could decline."

"You must read this book, Bud. Right now I'd better stop talking and hit the trail. I'll come by jeep, so I can bring along the fresh tanks of helium."

"Swell! See you soon, skipper," Bud said, and signed off.

The minutes dragged by slowly as he and Chow waited for Tom to appear. The Texan passed the time by whittling a wooden doll for Ahau Quetzal's little daughter.

It was almost two hours later when they heard the roar of a jeep's engine in the distance. "Here comes Tom!" Bud exclaimed.

He decided to take a short cut through the jungle and meet his approaching pal on the trail. Bud plunged among the trees but had gone only a short distance when he stopped short with a startled cry.

"The giant!" Bud gulped, as a huge, hairy, half-naked white man loomed out of the tangled shrubbery, blocking the boy's path. He was clad only in a loincloth, with sandals made of palm fibers. His long flowing hair hung down to his shoulders.

Seeing Bud's horrified look, the man threw back his head and gave a deep booming laugh. As Bud stepped back, seeking to dodge out of his way, the giant reached out and grabbed up the husky young flier as if he were a baby. Supporting him on the palm of one huge hand, the giant spun Bud around.

"Now you are the slave of the King of the Jungle!" the man roared in English.

"Cut it out! Let me down!" Bud yelled. He squirmed frantically in an effort to free himself, but the giant clutched him in a viselike grip!

"Okay, you asked for it!" Bud gritted. Twining both hands in the giant's flowing locks, Bud yanked the man's hair until he yelped with pain. He promptly loosened his hold and Bud jumped to the ground.

To Bud's surprise, the giant seemed to bear him no ill will over the hair-pulling. Instead, he gave another of his bellowing laughs. "Nice going, young fellow!" the giant said, patting Bud on the shoulder with a ham-sized hand. "I respect anyone as brave as you! Weren't frightened a bit, were you?"

At that moment Chow came running up, alarmed by the yells and the sounds of a struggle. He stopped short at sight of the giant. "G-great jumpin' Jehoshaphat!" Chow stuttered, his jaw sagging open.

"Don't worry," Bud assured him. "The guy's friendly—I *think*."

Before the giant could comment, Tom's jeep

came into view. Several Mayan men were trotting alongside, but one look at the giant sent them melting away into the jungle like shadows.

"Ho, ho, ho!" the huge man guffawed. "Look at 'em run! I terrify 'em!"

Tom braked the jeep to a halt and climbed out. "Just who are you?" he asked the giant.

"Maximilian Jones, that's me!" he answered, thumping himself on the chest. "Former heavyweight wrestler from California!"

"California?" Bud grinned. "Say, that's where I come from!"

"But I'm never going back," the giant added. "Not Max. No sirree!"

"Why not?" Tom asked.

"Because this jungle is the finest garden of health to be found on earth. You take it from me —I *know*. It made a new man out of me!"

"You mean you weren't always this big?" Bud asked.

"Sure, I was big," the ex-wrestler replied. "But I had a long siege of illness. Doctors couldn't do a thing for me. Then I came down here."

"Sounds like one of those 'Before and After' ads." Bud chuckled.

"Don't laugh—this is on the level," Max boomed. "I consulted a Mayan medicine man. He gave me some real potent stuff—herbs that he brewed himself. Had me back on my feet in no time! Of course the outdoor life helped too—that

"Now you are the slave of the King of the Jungle!"

and the wonderful native food. Between them all, they've turned me into a glowing picture of health!"

To emphasize his words, the ex-wrestler threw out his chest and flexed his mighty biceps. Tom barely managed to suppress a grin. He glanced quickly at his two companions. Bud responded with a wink, while Chow whispered out of the corner of his mouth:

"Punchy as a loco steer!"

Unfortunately, his words carried to Max. With a bellow of rage, the giant leaped at Chow!

CHAPTER VIII

THE SKINNY PHANTOM

TOM AND BUD hastily yanked Chow out of the way and stepped in front of the enraged giant.

"Hold on!" Tom commanded. "That's no way to treat a fellow American."

"Well, that ain't no way to *talk* about a fellow American, either," Max complained. "I heard what he said about me." The giant suddenly sounded like a sulky little boy. An injured look covered his broad pug face.

"I'm sure that Chow didn't mean any harm," Tom said soothingly, and the chef nodded emphatically. "Besides, we'd like to hear more about these health foods you've been eating down here."

Max brightened immediately and began to talk about the fruits, nuts, and roots that he lived on. From his enthusiasm, the boys realized that the ex-wrestler was not only crackbrained on the subject of health, but a food faddist of the most rabid kind.

Chow, who had been keeping a respectful distance from Max, now became interested. The cook was always eager to try out new concoctions. In the past he had served such unusual dishes as armadillo soup and whaleburgers. Perhaps some of the items Max mentioned might be worth trying, he thought.

Chow began questioning the giant and this seemed to please him immensely. Soon Max forgot his anger and became very friendly. "You fellows ought to come around and visit my cave some time," he boomed cheerfully.

"Do you really live in a cave?" Tom asked.

"Sure! Got it fixed up nice and homelike," Max boasted. "I even have a pet parrot and a lot of old relics."

Tom's eyes flashed with interest at mention of the relics. If they were of ancient Mayan workmanship, maybe some had space symbols like the sacred stone of Quetzal's tribe!

Meanwhile, Bud decided that he would risk a blunt question while the giant was in a good humor. "What were you doing skulking around our plane last night?" he asked boldly.

Max looked surprised. "Now, how'd you know that?" he exclaimed. "I'll bet someone snitched on me! That skinny little guy, eh? Well, it so happens I was chasing *him!*"

Tom and Bud looked at each other, mystified. "What skinny little guy?" Bud asked. "Someone from our camp? Or a native?"

"Search me." The wrestler shrugged. "It was dark and I got only a glimpse of a figure. I just wanted to get a look at your plane, that's all. Guess he did, too."

"What happened?" Tom put in.

"Nothing. When he spotted me, it must've scared the wits out of him!" Max guffawed at the recollection. "Anyhow, he went hightailing it off through the bush."

"Toward the Mayan village?" Tom went on.

"Nope. Now you mention it, he headed in a different direction—over that way." The giant pointed north.

Tom and Bud mulled over this information thoughtfully. Chow was still staring at the bare-chested strong man with keen interest.

"Aren't you skeered o' jaguars?" the cook asked.

"Jaguars?" Max laughed scornfully. "Naw! I just kill 'em with my bare hands!" He went through the motions of crushing a jaguar.

Chow clucked in amazement. "Brand my coyote cutlets, I sure wouldn't want to live down here for good with all them wild varmints runnin' around loose. I mean, it jest ain't safe!"

This seemed to rouse the wrestler's curiosity about Tom's group. "What're you fellows doing here in the jungle, anyway?" he asked.

"We're interested in studying the old Mayan stone carvings," Tom said cautiously. "I'd like to see some of your relics if we get a chance. Maybe we'll take you up on that invitation to visit your cave."

"Sure, you do that!" the giant boomed. "Any time! It's over that way." He jerked his thumb toward the east, then gave each one a resounding slap on the shoulder. Bud and Tom winced, while Chow's knees almost buckled.

"Well, so long, fellows! See you later!" With a parting wave, the giant strode off into the bush.

The three watched, more impressed than ever with his towering physique and bulging muscles, until he disappeared from view.

"Some build, I'll say that for his diet!" Tom commented.

Bud grinned and cupped his hands as if making a loud-speaker announcement: "Beware, all jaguars! Here comes Magnificent Max! This man is dangerous!"

Tom laughed. "Better hope he didn't hear that, pal! He doesn't seem to like having people make fun of him!"

"Do you suppose that guy is really as zany as he sounds?" Bud asked.

"Good question," Tom reflected, growing serious again. "I'd also like to know if he was telling the truth about seeing that 'skinny guy.' Either one of them could have tampered with our helium tanks. Which reminds me, I brought the new ones. Let's install them in the ship right now."

"Roger!" Bud agreed eagerly.

Tom drove the jeep as close to the paraplane as he could maneuver. Then, with the aid of a ramp and parbuckle sling, they hoisted the heavy tanks aboard and jettisoned the old ones.

"So far, so good." Tom laid aside the wrench he had used to connect the helium feed line, and wiped the sweat off his forehead. "Let's try the engine."

Bud nodded. "I was going to suggest that."

The young inventor warmed up the jet engine, checked various instrument readings, and gunned the throttle enough to make sure that everything was functioning properly.

To discourage further tampering with the helium supply, Tom padlocked the tank compartment. Then the three climbed into the jeep and headed back to the Mayan village.

As they jounced along over the jungle path, Bud asked, " How soon do we get a peek at your camera, Tom? I'm keen to see how it works."

"You'll get your chance in an hour or so," Tom replied. "Dick Folsom and Jack Murray are bringing it over here by truck."

"By truck?" Bud looked surprised.

Tom nodded. "I forgot we'd be needing one to haul the equipment, but Dad didn't, lucky for us! He shipped along a husky one-ton job with heavy-duty tires. It'll come in handy in this jungle country."

"How big is this camera contraption o' yours?" Chow asked curiously.

"Too big," Tom admitted, "even with my new miniaturized scanner. But I'm sure I can design a more compact model after we've tested my first retroscope thoroughly."

The Americans were greeted by a swarm of smiling, chattering Mayan children as Tom's jeep pulled into the village.

Chow said he would start off at once to attend to his cooking chores. "Reckon I'd better start thinkin' about supper," he explained.

"So soon?" Tom asked.

Chow's tanned, leathery face broke into a mysterious smile. "Wal now, seein' as how we got guests comin', I think it might be right friendly to greet 'em with a real native feast, don't you?"

"It might," Tom conceded, grinning, "as long as you don't go *too* native."

"No stewed jungle ants, please!" Bud added hastily, putting on a horrified look.

"Don't you worry, Buddy boy," the chef replied. "You jest leave the menu to old Chow Winkler, the best chuck-wagon cook what ever came out o' the Lone Star State!"

Chuckling to himself, the paunchy Westerner clumped off in his high-heeled boots. He had been really inspired by Magnificent Max's talk of jungle health foods, and wanted to try his own hand at native cookery.

Left to themselves, Tom and Bud strolled about the village. "Where do you plan to start using your camera?" Bud queried a few minutes later.

"We'll shoot all the stone carvings around here for traces of worn-off inscriptions," Tom decided. "Then I'll try probing underground and see if we can turn up any buried relics."

The boys passed an outdoor "kitchen" area where the women of the village had gathered to help prepare the feast. They were seated on the ground, patting the *zacan,* or ground corn, into round flat cakes on tiny three-legged wooden tables.

"*Uah,*" one woman said, pointing to the cakes.

Tom responded with a smile. "Must be the Mayan word for tortillas," he whispered.

"I'll make a note of it," Bud quipped.

Chow was crouched nearby, stirring a pan of dark-brown sauce. It was bubbling over a woodfire on a native "stove," which consisted of a metal tray set about six inches above the ground on stones.

"Jungle hot plate!" Bud commented.

Chow stirred busily, humming a cowboy song and pretending not to see the two boys.

"Come on. Let's leave the master to his work," Tom said with a chuckle.

He and Bud continued their stroll beyond the outskirts of the village. Here and there they came across a carved slab or half-crumbled stone column. All lay sunken deep in the jungle soil and overgrown with green, matted vegetation.

Tom examined each stone carefully. He also made various ground measurements, trying to locate mounds which might indicate a site of buried relics.

"How old do you suppose this carving is?" Bud asked as he scraped away some of the jungle growth from one of the stone slabs.

Tom shrugged. "No telling. Most of the known carvings date from after A.D. 300. But the Mayas lived in Central America for two or three thousand years before that.

"Speaking of time"—Tom glanced at his wrist watch with a worried look—"I wonder what's keeping the truck? Let's see if we can raise the men on the radio."

The two boys hurried back to the jeep. Tom hoisted its radio antenna and warmed up the transmitter. "Tom Jr. calling Dick Folsom and Jack Murray!" he said over the mike.

Repeated calls brought no response.

"Maybe they're not tuned in," Bud suggested.

"They should be," Tom said with a puzzled frown. "Bud, I think we'd better go find out if they're in trouble. I'd sure hate to have anything happen to them or my electronic retroscope either."

Tom notified Chow where they were going, then went to tell Chief Quetzal their plans. The young inventor had started thinking of various unexplained happenings. "Our friends may need help, so Bud and I will go and see what's wrong. And could you have two men guard our airplane while we're gone?"

The chief nodded. But his face grew grave when Tom mentioned that the truck was carrying a camera.

"Maybe your friends tried to take some pictures of Indians they met," Quetzal said slowly. "Some Indians do not like this. They fear their souls are being taken away. If that happened"—the chief shrugged—"your friends would indeed be in great danger."

Bud flashed his pal a look of alarm and Tom's eyes widened in dismay.

"Come on, Bud!" he cried out. "Let's get going!"

CHAPTER IX

A MAYAN FEAST

MAKING a dash to the jeep, Tom and Bud hopped in. Tom slid behind the wheel, flicked the starter, and threw the car into gear. But the engine merely coughed and died.

With a mutter of annoyance, Tom pressed the starter again, keeping his foot on the gas pedal. This time there was barely a sputter.

"Oh, fine!" Bud exploded. "What's wrong?"

"Search me," Tom said, trying again and again to gun the engine into life. "Battery's okay. Let's hope it's not vapor lock!" He climbed out, adding, "Slide over to the driver's seat while I take a look under the hood."

The young inventor checked the ignition and found that the plugs were sparking properly. He also disconnected the feed line briefly to make sure that the fuel pump was squirting gasoline to the carburetor.

"What's the dope?" Bud asked.

"Maybe the carburetor's fouled up," Tom conjectured. "Wait a second." He loosened the clamp and lifted off the air cleaner, then cupped the palm of his hand over the intake to help the suction. "Now try it."

This time, when Bud pressed the starter, the engine roared to life. But when Tom replaced the air cleaner, the motor died again.

"Maybe *I'm* nuts!" Tom exclaimed, puzzled.

Bud, also mystified, climbed from behind the steering wheel. He watched as Tom took the air cleaner apart. Moments later, both burst into laughter. A huge jungle insect with wings like parchment had been sucked into the cleaner and was clogging the central air tube!

"No wonder the jeep wouldn't start." Bud chuckled. "It had butterflies in its stomach!"

"May have been a butterfly once, but it sure is a mess now." Tom grinned as he tossed the oil-soaked insect aside.

Hastily he reassembled the cleaner, replaced it on the engine, and clamped the hood. Wiping his hands as best he could on the coarse vegetation, Tom slid back into the driver's seat and Bud climbed in beside him. In a matter of seconds, they were gunning off through the jungle.

Both boys grew tense and anxious again as Tom drove at top speed, grasping the wheel hard to keep the jeep from jouncing off the trail. Ten minutes later Bud gave a cry of alarm as he spotted the missing truck.

"They've cracked up!"

The vehicle had foundered in a half-hidden patch of bog. Both right wheels were deeply mired in the swampy muck, and the truck was listing at a crazy angle. Dick Folsom waved a gloomy greeting. He was standing alone at the scene of the accident.

"Where's Jack?" Tom cried anxiously, as he braked the jeep and jumped out.

"Went back to the *Sky Queen* for the crane tank," Dick replied. "The jolt knocked out our radio, so we couldn't signal for help."

Bud gave a whistle of dismay as he surveyed the damage. "You're lucky the truck didn't go over all the way!"

"Bad enough as it is," Dick said ruefully. "I'm afraid your retroscope is ruined, Tom." Part of the camera equipment had spilled out and lay in a tangled mass on the ground. Apparently Dick had been trying to salvage it when the jeep arrived.

"It doesn't matter," Tom said, fighting to keep a brave face in spite of his sickening disappointment. "The important thing is that you and Jack are okay."

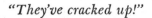

"They've cracked up!"

"How about me going after him in the jeep?" Bud suggested. "Maybe I can give him a lift part way."

As Bud drove off, the other two set about the laborious job of reassembling the spilled equipment. Dick, who was still unfamiliar with Tom's new scanner, could offer only limited help. To make matters worse, many of the delicate electronic parts had been wrenched loose or smashed. Tom worked patiently to salvage what he could and put his invention even partially in order.

"Jack feels as bad as I do, skipper," Dick said glumly. "We know how much you were counting on using the retroscope."

"Forget it." Tom managed a cheerful grin. "Maybe it's not as bad as we thought."

"Jack's going to bring back a supply of replacement parts and test gear," Dick added. "We figured there might be a faint hope of repairing the camera."

"Good. I'm sure we can fix it."

Half an hour later a small but powerful tank with a turret-mounted crane rumbled up to the scene. Bud and Jack Murray waved from inside the cab window. As the tank's caterpillar treads ground to a halt, the two passengers climbed out.

"One thing's sure," Bud announced with a chuckle. "There's now a clear trail between here and the Flying Lab. Boy, *nothing* stops this baby!" He patted the tank fondly.

"With built-in air conditioning!" Jack added. "You and your dad designed these tanks for the expedition to Little Luna, didn't you? But they're pretty handy here on earth, too—especially in a spot like this."

"What's the verdict on your camera?" Bud asked, as he eyed the reassembled equipment.

"With luck, we'll have it working okay," Tom assured him. "I doubt if the brain or reproducing unit was damaged much. It's mostly the scanning rig that needs repair."

"Hope I've brought everything you'll need," Jack said.

"We'll worry about that later," Tom told him. "Right now, let's get this truck and retroscope back on the road."

The tank's crane soon hoisted the truck out of the mire. Under Tom's supervision, the perspiring workers loaded the equipment aboard and made everything secure.

"Where now?" Bud asked. "The *Sky Queen?*"

Tom made a hasty check of the repair parts and other gear that Jack Murray had brought. "No, let's go on to the village," he decided. "I believe I can overhaul the camera there."

"How about the tank?" Jack inquired.

Tom grinned. "We'll bring it along and give the natives a motor show."

The procession started off through the rain forest. Tom, driving the tank, took the lead. Jack and

Dick followed in the truck, with Bud bringing up the rear in the jeep. All wore headphones and kept their radios tuned in order to communicate freely with one another.

A constant din assaulted the travelers' ears as the cavalcade plowed its way through the jungle. Monkeys chattered angrily from the overhanging tree branches, while bright-colored parrots and macaws screeched in protest. Every few minutes a fresh covey of birds would flutter skyward, alarmed by the rattle and rumble of the vehicles.

"Boy, an enemy plane could spot us from miles away!" Dick commented with a chuckle.

Weary and hungry, the group finally reached the Mayan village. News of their approach had spread, and Ahau Quetzal and his whole tribe had assembled to stare in awe as the travelers climbed out of their steel caravan.

"First you drop from sky in strange airship," Quetzal told Tom. "Now you come in a steel monster which crawls along the ground like a lizard or snake. You are indeed possessed of great magic!"

Tom smiled and shook his head. "Not magic. Like your great Mayan ancestors who ruled here in Yucatan, I study science—meaning the laws of nature. My father taught me that those laws must be used only for the good of mankind."

"Then he too must be a wise man," said Quetzal, nodding approvingly.

"Now that *that's* over—*come an' get it!*" Chow bawled.

He stepped from the crowd, banging a native gong. Then the cook turned to Wilson Hutchcraft, who had just languidly entered the village. "You're invited too, pardner!"

In the center of the clearing the women had spread large ferns for a "table." At each place was a crude mat woven from the leaves of the guano palm. The "dishes" were fashioned from hollowed-out pieces of a banana-tree trunk. As the men and children scrambled for places, the women served the delicious native food.

First course for the North Americans was mamee—a sweet, red-meated fruit. Next, Chow served a steaming platter of stewed chicken, covered with a rich dark-brown sauce.

"Mm!" Bud closed his eyes and inhaled the appetizing aroma. Then he added, pointing to the sauce, "But what's this stuff?"

"It's called *molé*," Chow exclaimed proudly. "Somethin' special—made out o' chocolate an' spices. The womenfolk showed me how to whip it up. You jest taste it!"

The Americans were a bit dubious about the idea of combining chocolate sauce with chicken. But after sampling a few bites of the dish, they fell to avidly.

"Sounds crazy," Jack Murray remarked between bites, "but it tastes wonderful!"

The chicken was accompanied by side dishes of tortillas, baked native squash, called chayote, and a sort of raw turnip, jicama. For dessert, the feast was topped off with avocados and oranges.

"Chow, old boy, you've done us proud!" Bud said as he sat back and loosened his belt.

"One of the best meals I ever ate," Tom agreed, and Chow grinned.

When the remains of the feast had been cleared away, Ahau Quetzal clapped his hands to call for music. A dozen of the Mayan men brought out drums, gourd rattles, wooden flutes, and other instruments. Then a group of native dancers came forward, balancing bottles, crocks, and jugs on top of their flat, broad heads.

"What in tarnation is all the crockery for?" Chow wondered. The others from Shopton were equally mystified.

The answer soon became evident. As the musicians played a gay Spanish tune, the dancers whirled and stepped without disturbing the articles on their heads. Evidently it was a mark of skill to keep the objects balanced.

"Hey, they're good!" Dick exclaimed, clapping his hands in time to the music.

By now, it was deep twilight and the blazing fire that had been built to celebrate the feast made the scene even more colorful. Chow watched in grinning admiration. Finally some of the dancers beckoned him to join in.

"Go on, Chow! Show 'em a Texas reel!" Bud urged. "And don't forget your headpiece!" Seizing a large clay water jug, he placed it on the cook's head.

Chow, full of enthusiasm, needed little urging. He waddled out among the dancers, balancing the jug precariously. Soon the chef was dancing a lively jig.

"What a man!" Bud roared, as he and the rest of Tom's group shook with laughter.

Puffing and panting, Chow edged closer to his friends to show off his skill. But the jug was wobbling more and more wildly. Suddenly, as Chow reached up to steady it, the jug arced from his head.

"Look out!" Tom cried. He made a wild grab for the heavy jug but missed. It struck Hutchcraft squarely in the forehead!

With a groan, Hutchcraft reeled under the impact, then slumped to the ground, unconscious!

CHAPTER X

BALL OF MAGIC

THE MUSIC came to an abrupt stop and the crowd gasped as they stared at Hutchcraft's motionless form.

Chow wrung his hands. "Brand my stupid ole hide, this is terrible!"

"Wasn't your fault—just a freakish accident," Tom tried to calm him. "I'm sure that Hutch isn't seriously hurt." As the Mayas clustered around to lend sympathy, he added in Spanish, "Give him air, please!"

With Bud's help, Tom lifted the unconscious victim to a more comfortable spot. Chow bustled off to bring some cloths soaked in cool water, which had just been brought from the village well.

An ugly bruise and swelling were appearing on Hutchcraft's temple. After several applications of cold compresses, however, the Bostonian revived. He sat up with a groan, then scowled as he caught sight of Chow. "Of all the dirty tricks!" Hutch-craft exclaimed.

"Dirty tricks!" The softhearted Westerner was horrified. "You ain't thinkin' I beaned you with that jug on purpose, are you?"

"Don't pretend to be innocent," Hutchcraft retorted. "If you don't like me, say so! But you don't have to try fracturing my skull!"

"Maybe it could still be arranged," Bud muttered, bristling with anger. Both he and Tom were indignant at Hutchcraft's attitude.

Nevertheless, Tom nudged Bud for silence before the copilot's quick temper made matters worse. "You can see from Chow's face how bad he feels about the accident," Tom told Hutchcraft evenly. "We're all sorry it happened, and there's no reason to make unfair accusations."

Meanwhile, the *ahmen,* the native medicine man, was doing his bit for the injured man. Having seen Hutchcraft lying unconscious, he had hurried to don his parrot-feather headdress and other regalia. Now he glided back and forth with slow, dancing steps, all the while waving a small greenish stone ball over the archaeologist's head. This was accompanied by a singsong chant.

Hutchcraft glared at him in annoyance. "Confounded native mumbo-jumbo!" he fumed. "Go on—clear out! Leave me alone!" Waving his arms threateningly, he chased the medicine man away.

A shocked murmur arose from the villagers.

The Americans, embarrassed by Hutchcraft's show of bad temper, coldly walked away from him.

Tom was too interested in the ahmen's medicine ball to waste further words on Hutchcraft. The curious-looking green stone had caught the young scientist's eye. He hurried after the medicine man and asked if he might see it.

The medicine man hesitated. "It is a *sastun,* used for making strong magic," he explained. But finally he allowed Tom to examine the ball. It was a perfect sphere, about two inches in diameter, made of polished jade. "What beautiful workmanship!" Tom exclaimed admiringly. The surface of the ball was inscribed with delicate carvings.

Tom took out his pocket magnifying glass and tried to decipher some of the pictographs. But they were too worn and faint from being handled.

"Must be centuries old!" Tom thought excitedly. Aloud, he asked the medicine man if he might test the jade ball to determine its age.

"Even I cannot tell you when it was made," the medicine man replied. "This sastun has been passed down by my father's father and by many generations before him. No one knows its age."

"I have a special machine which may help us find out how old it is," Tom replied. He pointed to the camera equipment in the truck, parked nearby. "Would you let me try?"

Impressed by Tom's explanation, the medicine man agreed. But suddenly he held up his hand. "Wait!" After sniffing the air, he announced, "I smell rain. A bad storm is coming. I must warn the villagers!"

The medicine man's forecast seemed unbelievable. The stars were out and the sky almost cloudless. But maybe the man had a sixth sense, Tom thought. Rather than take a chance exposing the retroscope to bad weather, Tom asked for help in unloading his equipment.

The heavy gear had hardly been moved into Quetzal's hut when rain came down in torrents. Tom and the others talked for a while, then climbed into their hammocks, glad of their snug quarters. The rain, beating on the hut's thatched roof, soon lulled them to sleep.

The next morning after breakfast Tom set to work checking and repairing his retroscope. To his delight, he found that neither the electronic brain nor the reproducing unit had suffered serious damage. Dick Folsom and Jack Murray offered to do the minor repairs needed on these units, so Tom gladly turned over that part of the job to the two engineers.

"How about the rest of your rig?" Bud asked.

"I'm afraid that it will take some time to fix," Tom replied. He unscrewed the casing of the scanning camera, exposing the smashed and tangled electronic assembly inside. "I hate to tackle it! Won't be hard, though—just a lot of fine, tedious benchwork."

"Wish I could help, but that glunk throws me," Bud confessed. "Maybe I'd better go check on the paraplane."

"Good idea," Tom said. "But watch yourself, pal! Don't let that skinny snooper Max told us about make a sitting duck out of you."

Bud promised to observe caution, and set off in the jeep. In the meantime, Chow was busy on a project of his own. The old Texan had organized a crew of Quetzal's tribesmen to build a special hut for Tom Swift's group, so that the chief could return to his own quarters.

"You are thoughtful!" the chief said when Chow had asked his approval.

First the tribesmen scattered into the forest with axes and machetes to cut and trim the necessary timber. Quetzal himself chose each piece with the skilled, loving eye of a craftsman.

After he had marked out a site at one end of the village, a series of stakes were driven into the ground. These were of young sapodilla wood and formed the walls of the hut. The stakes were tied together with palm fibers and daubed with a thick coating of mud.

"Don't you ever use hammer and nails?" Chow asked, puzzled.

Quetzal broke into one of his rare smiles. "I

have seen such tools once when I was in Mérida," he replied. "But we Mayas have no need of them."

Meanwhile, other native workmen were laying floor planks of mahogany and Spanish cedar. A framework was then raised to support the ridge-pole and thatching of the roof.

"Brand my fryin' pan," Chow reflected, "when it comes to slappin' a house together fast, these little folks really know their business!"

Tom was busily at work assembling various transistors and other parts in the main detector eye when Bud drove up in the jeep.

"How goes it?" he asked.

"Almost finished," Tom replied. "Dick and Jack have the other units ready. I just have the hookup to do and a little adjusting. How about the ship?"

"Everything seems okay," Bud reported. "No sign of the skinny man, either."

"Swell! Now if my camera works, we're in business!"

Tom had just finished checking out the whole setup when Chow came clumping into the hut, followed by Quetzal. Both were beaming mysteriously.

"Got somethin' to show you, boss!" the old ranch cook announced. "Come along an' see!"

Tom, Bud, and the two engineers trooped after him, curious to find out what was up. They stared in amazement when Chow showed them the spanking new hut, larger than any other in the village.

"You mean it's ours?" Tom gasped.

"Sí, amigo," the chief replied. "A present from my people to our friends from the Estados Unidos!"

Touched, Tom made a short speech of thanks and said he would move the retroscope there later. Then Tom announced that he would try at once to make a photograph with his special camera to discover how the faint carving on the medicine man's jade ball had looked originally.

This time it was Chow's turn to be astonished. He asked Tom to explain.

"You mean that contraption o' yours kin take a picture o' what somethin' looked like a long time ago?" Chow asked.

"That's why I call my invention a 'retroscope,' " Tom replied. "The name is formed from Greek and Latin words meaning to 'see back.' "

Chow asked with a grin, "Could it make a picture o' me back when I was a handsome young feller with a full head o' hair?"

Everyone burst out laughing.

"I'll be satisfied if it does the trick on these Mayan stones," Tom replied.

The natives were so curious that Tom agreed to move his retroscope setup outside Quetzal's hut where all could watch. Then he switched on the power supply, consisting of several Swift solar batteries hooked to a small motor-generator unit.

As the equipment warmed up, Tom tuned various dials and trained the scanner eyes on the jade ball. Presently a magnified picture of the old Mayan pictographs began to form on the reproducer screen.

Gasps of delight rose from the natives, who crowded closer for a better look. Their awe increased, a moment later, when Tom flicked a lever and pulled a photographic film from the machine showing the same design pattern.

Though the picture was far from clear, Tom was able to make out a set of Mayan numerals, giving the date when the sastun was made. He read this off to Quetzal: *9.4.0.0.0 13 Ahau 18 Yax.*

"What's that in our calendar?" Dick asked.

"October 18, A.D. 514," Tom translated. Turning to Quetzal, he added, "More than three baktuns ago."

The chief's eyes widened. "Truly, my people have lived here a long time!"

"We can't be sure the stone was carved here in your village, Ahau," Tom pointed out. "Even your sacred stone may have been brought here by people other than your ancestors."

As simply as he could, Tom explained that it would be necessary to dig up local stone carvings. These would then have to be deciphered, time-checked, and compared with the sastun and sacred stone to find out if they were made by the same people.

Just as Tom finished speaking, Hutchcraft walked up to the hut. He was holding a rather muddy rock, which he held out to Tom. "Looks as if this has some markings on it," the Bostonian said. "See what your time machine can make out."

Tom was doubtful that the rock had ever borne any carvings. But rather than offend Hutchcraft, he placed it in front of the camera and switched on power. The set hummed into operation, but no picture formed on the screen.

Instead, the rock suddenly exploded, showering the onlookers with shrapnellike pieces of debris!

CHAPTER XI

A NARROW ESCAPE

CRIES and groans went up from the natives. Many had been hit by flying bits of rock. Bud was bleeding from a cut on the cheek, and Dick Folsom had been grazed on the forehead.

"Brand my flyin' flapjacks, what was in that stone?" Chow gasped in bewilderment. "A charge o' blastin' powder?"

"I sure wouldn't be surprised!" Bud snapped, dabbing his cheek with a handkerchief. "Maybe our helpful friend here can tell us!" He clenched his fists angrily and started toward Hutchcraft.

"Take it easy, pal!" Tom said, stopping him. "We have enough trouble already."

"Thanks to Hutchcraft!" Bud stormed. "If you ask me, he knew this would happen!"

The Bostonian looked pale and somewhat frightened by the havoc he had caused. But before he could answer Bud's charges, Tom intervened.

"We'll talk about that later," the young scientist

said firmly. "Right now, it's more important to help these people who have been hurt!"

Jack Murray and Chow were sent to bring first-aid kits from the vehicles. Meanwhile, Tom and Ahau Quetzal did their best to calm the excited Mayas.

Fortunately, the only injuries were minor cuts and bruises. As Tom applied antiseptic and bandages, the superstitious victims began to calm down.

When the situation was finally under control, Tom turned back to Hutchcraft. "Where did that stone come from?" he demanded.

"It wasn't really a carved stone," Hutchcraft admitted sheepishly. "I found it in your truck, and thought I'd play a trick on you."

"Fine trick!" Bud growled. "I suppose if someone had lost an eye, you'd be laughing your head off!"

"I didn't know the thing would explode!" Hutchcraft said sulkily. "I only wanted to get even for Chow's nasty attack on me last night. I thought I could fool you fellows into believing your machine wouldn't work. Just a harmless prank, that's all."

Bud received his lame excuses with a snort of disgust.

Tom picked up what was left of the stone. He examined it, together with several of the exploded fragments. "You say you found this in our truck?" he asked Hutchcraft.

The Bostonian nodded. "It looked like an ordinary stone. I assumed it was something you'd used to prop up your equipment."

"It's a form of mica, hydrous silicate," Tom said. "Must have been dumped into the truck on a hauling job back in Shopton. I guess that explains its blowing up."

"How come?" Bud asked, still suspicious.

"This stuff breaks down under radiation," Tom explained. "It must have absorbed too much output from the camera and exploded. The pieces that hit us are now vermiculite."

Bud and the others were mollified, so Tom resumed his retroscope test. Several other stones were "photographed." But in every case the picture was far from clear.

"That's worse'n my old TV set, boss," said Chow, squinting his eyes. "Can't you tune it any sharper?"

"I'm afraid not, Chow," Tom said with a rueful grin. "The camera's discrimination just isn't good enough."

Chow scratched his bald head. "Reckon I'll have to take your word for it."

"What I mean is, the camera is being thrown off by outside radiation," Tom explained.

"Such as?" put in Bud.

"Such as high-level atomic fallout and cosmic radiation reaching the earth from outer space. My retroscope detectors are only supposed to pick up the radioactivity from the rock itself. But the trouble is that they're also picking up this outside radiation, too."

"I get it—the camera can't tell which is which." Bud grinned and added, "What this job needs are bifocals!"

Tom winced in mock horror at his pal's joke. "I wish it were that simple."

"Perhaps you can design something to shield out the other radiation," Jack Murray suggested.

Tom shook his head doubtfully. "I'm afraid it's too intense for any effective shielding."

After mulling over the matter, the young inventor decided to return to the *Sky Queen* and work on the problem in his private laboratory. "I'll fly back in the paraplane," he told the others. "How about you fellows staying here to guard the retroscope?"

"Sure, boss. Don't you worry about a thing," Chow assured him, as all agreed. "We'll fix it so there's someone here ridin' herd on your camera all the time."

"Swell. And keep the tank radio tuned," Tom added.

Hopping into the jeep, Tom drove to the spot where the parachute plane was berthed. There was no sign that the ship had been tampered with by marauders. "Better try the engine, anyhow, before I take off," he thought cautiously.

The young inventor eased into the pilot's seat

and gunned the jet engine into life. But after a loud, blasting sputter, it died. Tom tried again but got no response.

"Now what's wrong?" he wondered in annoyance.

He climbed out of the plane and made a quick check of the engine. Then he inspected the main fuel tank. To his disgust the drainage from the pump showed considerable water in the fuel.

"Oh, great!" Tom fumed. "This plane seems to be jinxed! That downpour last night probably flooded the fuel system."

For a moment Tom considered using gasoline from the ground vehicles. But he quickly discarded this idea, since the paraplane's power plant had been designed for special jet fuel.

"Guess I'll have to drive to the Flying Lab by jeep," Tom decided. Before leaving, he contacted the village by radio.

Bud answered. "What's up, pal?" When Tom reported his plight, Bud commented, "Maybe it wasn't just the rain!"

"Meaning what?" Tom asked.

"Meaning that skinny guy Max told us about," Bud replied. "He may have dumped water into the tank on purpose. I think we should do some detective work and try to get a line on that skinny joker—or at least find out if Magnificent Max just dreamed up the whole thing."

"Maybe you've got something there," Tom

agreed. "We'll talk about it when I get back."

Tom signed off and made everything secure aboard the paraplane. Then he climbed into the jeep again and started off on the long, grueling trail to the Flying Lab.

The towering trees of the tropical rain forest shut out the sunlight, and the dark, steamy atmosphere was noisy with the buzz of insects and the raucous screams of jungle birds. "This is sure no place for a picnic!" Tom thought wryly.

Suddenly a scream of terror reached his ears. Tom slammed on the brakes, his face turning pale at the agonized sound. "Good grief! What was that?" he wondered.

Again he heard screaming. "That's a human voice!" Tom realized. Grabbing the rifle which

The beast came whirling down
and charged straight at Tom

had been carried in the jeep at all times since the Flying Lab's arrival, Tom leaped out and ran toward the sound.

The terrified shrieks grew louder as he fought his way through the tangled ferns and underbrush. A moment later, at a spot hemmed in by dense growth and rocks, Tom burst upon a frightening scene. A man lay unconscious on the ground. Over him reared a huge jaguar, its claws ready for the kill. The man had evidently cornered the jaguar and infuriated it.

Tom had no choice but to shoot the animal. He had to save the man. Whipping his rifle to his shoulder, he fired at the beast.

It leaped into the air and came down whirling to face its new enemy. Though wounded, the jaguar was snarling with fury—still full of fight! It charged straight at Tom!

The young inventor's heart was hammering, but he kept cool. Dropping on one knee, he took aim and fired again, point-blank.

It was a clean hit! But the enraged animal refused to go down. Instead, the jaguar seemed to gain strength from its added fury at being wounded a second time. The beast charged again.

With sweating hands, Tom leveled the rifle for another shot. But the hammer merely clicked on an empty chamber. His gun was empty!

CHAPTER XII

THE WRESTLER'S CAVE

TOM gave way to an instant of blind panic. But it was gone in a flash as he realized that his life depended on split-second action!

Flinging his rifle aside, Tom dashed for the nearest tree—a towering Spanish cedar. He grabbed the trunk in a flying leap and hauled himself clear of the ground not a second too soon!

As Tom shinned upward, the maddened jaguar almost grazed his leg with a lightning sweep of one paw. Tom shuddered—those terrible claws would have ripped his flesh to the bone!

Shivering with relief and drenched in cold perspiration, Tom lodged himself on a tree branch and waited for his heart to stop pounding. "I hope that cat will die soon," he thought sympathetically, "but I'm sure not coming down while it's still alive!"

Tom had only a few seconds to wait. The jaguar sank to the ground and flopped over on one side.

Cautiously Tom climbed down for a closer look. There was no doubt but that the beast was dead. "He's a beauty. I wish I hadn't had to kill him."

Picking up his empty rifle, Tom hurried toward the unconscious man on the ground. "It's Magnificent Max!" the young inventor realized with concern.

The long-haired giant lay sprawled in a clumsy heap. As Tom reached his side, the ex-wrestler stirred and moaned, then sat up and looked at his rescuer.

"Where am I?" Max mumbled. As his brain cleared, his eyes fell on the dead jaguar. "Oh, yeah . . . I remember now. I was having a fight with that man-killer!"

Heaving himself to his feet, with Tom's help, the giant threw out his chest proudly. "Man, what a terrific struggle!" he gasped. "That jaguar went straight for my throat! But I finally killed him, with nothing but my bare hands!"

"Now just a minute, fellow," Tom said quietly. "Don't you think this cave-man bit has gone far enough? I killed that jaguar with a couple of shots. You were out cold."

Max's face fell sheepishly. "Okay, so I like to talk big," he muttered. "Guess I'm just trying to build myself up. . . . You've got to admit, though, that man-killer never hurt me a bit!"

"You were just lucky," Tom replied. "I think all that yelling you did must have unnerved the jaguar. Then, when he finally closed in on you, you fainted."

"Well, anyhow"—Max thrust out a huge hand and shook Tom's in a bone-crushing grip—"I'm glad you came along. Guess I won't corner a jaguar again! Thanks for saving my life!"

"Forget it," Tom responded with a smile. "I'm sure you'd have done the same in my place."

"You bet your boots I would!" the giant boomed. "Say, how about dropping over to my cave for that visit we were talking about? It's not far from here."

Tom hesitated. Although the jungle strong man seemed genuinely grateful and friendly, Tom still did not trust him completely. To keep from appearing rude, the young inventor explained that right now he was in a hurry to reach the expedition's laboratory plane.

"Suppose I stop in on my way back?" Tom suggested. Mentally he decided it might be wiser not to go to the cave alone with Max. "By the way," he added, "have you seen that skinny guy again?"

Max shook his head. "Nope, not since the night I chased him."

"If you do spot him around," Tom requested, "see if you can find out what he's up to."

"Don't worry. I'll shake the truth out of him!" The man gave another of his deep, bellowing laughs. "Well, see you later, pal!" He slapped Tom on the back, gave him another powerful handshake, and walked over to the dead jaguar. With a grunt, he slung the heavy carcass over one shoulder.

"Don't forget now. Come and see me," Max urged. He pointed out the cave's direction.

"I'll do that," Tom promised. He watched the giant stride off through the underbrush until he disappeared from view. "What a man!" he thought, chuckling.

Tom picked up the rifle and made his way back to the jeep. "I wonder what happened to this weapon. I fired only twice before running out of shells. But I was sure it was fully loaded before it was put in the jeep. And I'm positive I shoved in a full clip."

Puzzled, he climbed into the car and headed for the Flying Lab. When he reached it, Doc Simpson and the crewmen noticed Tom's disheveled appearance and the scratches he had received from climbing the cedar tree.

"Good grief, what have you been up to?" Doc exclaimed.

"Believe it or not, up a tree," Tom replied with a grin, and related his adventure.

Doc, horrified, felt that Tom should lie down and rest to recover from the strain of his narrow escape from death.

But the young inventor waved the suggestion aside. "I'm too busy, Doc—no kidding. I'll make up for it with a good sleep tonight."

Hurrying to the radio compartment, he called George Dilling at Enterprises. They chatted a few moments, then Dilling alerted Tom's father.

"How's everything, son?" Mr. Swift asked.

"Pretty well under control, Dad." Tom described the results obtained so far with his electronic retroscope and the need for more work on his invention. Then he asked, "How about our five little Mayan friends up there?"

"Doing fine at last report. They have one floor of a dorm at Grandyke University." Mr. Swift chuckled as he described the natives' reaction to North American civilization. "They've gone clothes crazy, especially about sport clothes. One of them goes around in a freshman cap and a bright purple polo shirt!"

Tom laughed and said, "I'm glad they're enjoying themselves."

"By the way, son," Mr. Swift went on, "you'll have some guests yourself soon. Sandy and Phyl are eager to see the Mayan village and watch your camera in operation, so I promised to fly them down. I want to see how your retroscope works too. We'll leave tomorrow night."

"Great, Dad!" Tom exclaimed. "I'll be looking for you. And by the way, that official from the Yucatan Institute, Señor Barancos, hasn't shown up yet."

Mr. Swift promised to check with the government authorities about the delay, then signed off.

The young inventor was smiling as he headed for his private laboratory. "It'll sure be swell to have Sandy and Phyl!" he thought. "Wait till I tell Bud." Tom's sister and her friend, Phyllis Newton, and the two boys had been a congenial foursome for years.

Once seated in his laboratory, however, Tom focused all his attention on his present task. Somehow, he must improve his retroscope's discrimination against outside radiation.

"A shield is no good," Tom mused, rumpling his crewcut absent-mindedly, "unless . . . unless I can figure a way to cancel out the interfering rays with some form of counterradiation."

Perhaps, he thought, his repelatron principle could be adapted to accomplish this. Tom turned the problem over and over in his mind, without seeing any glimmer of a solution. Then, suddenly, he snapped his fingers.

"Maybe I've solved it!" he thought excitedly. "Suppose I beam out a microwave field around the camera and use that as a screen, operating in connection with the computer!"

Actually, two fields would be necessary, he soon realized—one above the camera detectors and one below. Any radiation that passed through *both* fields would automatically "identify itself" as coming from the upper atmosphere. The electronic brain could be "ordered" to throw out such radiation.

On the other hand, all radiation coming from the object being photographed would pass *between* the two fields. The brain would use only this radiation in making its computations and thus produce a clear picture without interference.

Tom thumped his workbench. "I'm sure it will work!" Then he reflected ruefully, "But it will take some fancy circuit design to do all that without making the camera bigger and clumsier than ever!"

Using one of his midget desk computers, which Bud had nicknamed "Little Idiot," Tom quickly worked out the mathematical angles involved and dashed off rough sketches. Then he began building two compact transmitters with dish-shaped radiating antennas. These would be attached at the top and bottom of the camera.

Tom barely paused for supper and kept working hour after hour. At midnight Doc Simpson walked into the laboratory. "You promised to get a good sleep tonight, remember?" the medic reproved sternly.

Tom yawned, grinned, and laid down his electric drill. "Okay, Doc."

The next morning Tom quickly finished his two transmitter-radiator units, then called Bud over the ship's radio. "I'm starting back to the village, Bud. On the way, I intend to call on our friend, Magnificent Max. You can look for me around lunchtime."

"You think you can trust that overgrown herb eater?" Bud asked in concern.

"Don't worry. I'm not taking any chances." Tom chuckled. "I'll bring Frenchy along."

Frenchy Boudreau, a huge, rawboned Canadian from Quebec, had come to Swift Enterprises as a flight crewman after serving a hitch in the RCAF. He was the biggest man in the *Sky Queen's* crew.

As an added precaution, the young inventor gave Bud the approximate location of Max's cave.

Ten minutes later Tom and Frenchy started out in the jeep. When they reached the area where Tom had killed the jaguar, they left the jeep and struck off on foot into the tangled wilderness.

They found the cave without difficulty, and were greeted by loud squawks and screeches from Max's pet parrot perched in a tree near the entrance. Hearing the noise, Max came out.

"Oh, it's you, Junior!" the giant boomed, giving Tom one of his bone-crushing handshakes.

When he shook hands with Frenchy a moment later, the big flight crewman applied a little pressure of his own. Max winced and let go hastily. The Canadian merely smiled.

"I'd like to see some of those relics you were telling us about," Tom said.

"Sure, sure! Come in!" Max replied, leading the way.

The cave, which seemed to be very deep, was

partly lighted by a guttering candle stuck into
a porcelain bottle. Max's home contained a hammock, a low cookstove, a rough table and bench
hewn out of logs, and a jaguar rug. Much of the
living space was heaped with Mayan relics.

Tom gasped at sight of the treasure trove.
There were assorted items of pottery, carved stone
figures and animal representations which looked
as if they had once adorned the outside of a temple
or palace, and a number of metal ornaments such
as bracelets, arm bands, and necklaces.

"Good night! Where did you get all this?"
Tom asked.

The giant shrugged. "Oh, I found 'em in the
jungle or dug 'em up here and there. Some day I
may give 'em to a museum."

Tom wondered if his host was aware of the
Mexican government regulations about the finding of art treasures. All such objects were supposed
to be handed over to the civil authorities, who,
in turn, would pay the finder. But Tom decided
not to mention this now.

The young inventor examined a number of the
relics, one by one. Suddenly his eye fell on a per-
fectly shaped bowl. Tom picked it up and brought
it closer to the light. The bowl was covered with
faint carvings.

"This is important!" Tom thought, as he studied the carvings under his magnifying glass.
Though badly worn, they looked like the mathe-

matical symbols used by the Swifts' space friends
—the same as those which had been carved on the
sacred stone of Ahau Quetzal's tribe!

"Where did you find this bowl?" Tom asked.

Max looked at him a bit suspiciously before
answering. "You really want to know?"

"I certainly do!" Tom replied. "And I'll ap-
preciate it very much if you can show me the
place!"

"Okay." Max picked up the candle and headed
into the inky darkness of the cave's interior. "Follow me!" he muttered.

CHAPTER XIII

PARROT'S WARNING

COULD the ex-wrestler be trusted? Tom wondered. Or was Max planning to play some kind of trick on him and Frenchy after he had lured his visitors away from their only route of escape?

Frenchy flashed Tom a questioning look as if waiting for orders. Before the young inventor could decide, Max's parrot gave a loud screech. An instant later a familiar foghorn voice came bellowing into the cavern:

"Brand my stewed sombrero, what kind o' layout is this, anyhow?"

Tom gave a grin of relief as he saw Chow Winkler stomp into the cave in his high-heeled cowboy boots. Jack Murray entered behind the old Texan.

Max, who had turned to see the cause of the uproar, scowled at the new arrivals. He seemed none too pleased at this latest invasion of his cave.

If Chow noticed the giant's unfriendly look, he gave no sign. "We figgered you might like some company, Tom," the cook said. "So we jest hopped into the truck an' drove out to meet you."

"That was mighty thoughtful, Chow," Tom said, suppressing a smile. He introduced Jack Murray to the glowering jungle man, then added, "Max was just going to show me where he got some of these valuable relics. Maybe you fellows would like to come along."

"We certainly would," said Jack. "It sounds very interesting."

"Well . . . okay," Max grumbled. "But watch your step in here—it's rough going."

As the giant turned to lead the way, Tom signaled Frenchy to remain on guard at the cave entrance. Then he took out his powerful pocket flash and followed with the others.

When they had gone about fifty yards into the rocky interior, the cave suddenly narrowed into a mere passageway. Here the atmosphere became dank and almost chilly. The visitors plodded after Max in single file. Then, as they rounded a corner in the tunnel, it widened out again into another cavern.

A second later Chow gave a gasp of astonishment. The yellow light from Max's candle and Tom's flash had suddenly lit up a section of the cave wall, revealing the huge carved figure of a warrior!

"Great jumpin' mud frogs!" Chow gulped in a trembling voice. "Who's *that?*"

The figure was so lifelike and terrifying that it almost seemed to leap out of the wall at them. Chiseled out of limestone, the statue still showed traces of the gaudy colors in which it had once been painted.

The warrior had on a tall headdress of flowing quetzal feathers. His face was turned in profile, so that one huge eye glared out at the intruders. A jeweled spike through the nose just below the nostrils gave him added fierceness. In one hand he clutched a dying captive by the throat; in the other, a plumed serpent.

"That's the Mayan serpent god Kukulcan he's holding!" Tom exclaimed in awe.

Max brought his candle closer and stared at the carvings with the jealous, greedy look of a miser. "This is why I stay here," he said in a strange voice. "I discovered him and all the rest of the things. They're mine. Nobody can take them away from me!"

Tom exchanged a warning glance with his two companions. Jack winked and nodded, indicating that he and Chow would keep an eye on the jungle strong man in case he grew belligerent.

Reassured, Tom took the opportunity to study the wall relief more closely. "I believe these carvings date from sometime after the Old and New Mayan Empires," he told the others. "Some of the ornamentation has a Mexican look, which probably means the carvings were made after the Toltec invasion from the north."

"Then they're not so old after all?" Jack asked in surprise.

"Old enough," Tom replied. "Say, about the thirteenth century."

"Whew!" Jack gave a whistle. "That's seven hundred years ago. They're certainly well preserved."

Tom nodded. Inwardly, he was wondering if this section of the cave might be part of a buried temple. He decided that when Señor Barancos arrived, he would bring the government official to see this amazing archaeological find.

Meanwhile, Max had begun to claw away some loose dirt from the wall of the cave, to the left of the carved figure. "You ain't seen nothing yet!" he muttered.

The others watched with interest. Presently Max's digging exposed a gaping hole in the wall. Inside lay a heaping store of Mayan artifacts—bowls, jewelry, statuettes, and amulets.

Chow gasped as the flickering rays of Max's candle lit up the priceless objects. "Brand my buffalo chops, it's a reg'lar treasure room!" he declared.

Tom probed the darkened hollow with the beam of his flashlight. "You're right, Chow," he

"It's the Mayan serpent god, Kukulcan!"

said. "That's just what this is—a treasure chamber. It's been hewn out of solid rock!"

Max watched with a wary eye as Tom made a hasty survey of the hoard. None of the objects bore any mathematical space symbols. But one small carved figure of a turtle showed the date of A.D. 821 in Mayan numerals.

"This place may be older than I thought," Tom announced. "Of course many of these objects could have been made before the period of the wall carving and brought here."

"It's amazing—absolutely amazing," Jack declared. "I've never seen anything like it in my life."

When Tom had finished his examination, Max carefully heaped up the dirt again so as to cover his secret trove. Then the group started back through the narrow passageway leading to the outer room of the cave.

Frenchy was waiting patiently when they reached the giant's living quarters. "See anything interesting?" he asked with a grin.

"Pardner, we sure did!" Chow declared enthusiastically. The ex-ranch cook burst into a colorful, though confusing, description of the huge carved warrior and the hidden treasure chamber. "Enough to scare a law-abidin' hombre out of a year's growth."

Chow was interrupted by a sudden screech from the parrot. Max looked up, instantly alert. As the bird continued to squawk, his master made a dash toward the cave entrance.

"I'll bet an iguana there's some snooper out there!" the giant growled angrily.

Tom followed at his heels, with Jack Murray close behind. They emerged from the cave just in time to see the upper half of a slender figure disappearing among the ferns and foliage.

"That's him!" Max shouted. "That's the skinny guy I was telling you about!"

"Come on! After him!" Tom cried, starting off in pursuit.

CHAPTER XIV

FIGHTING MAD

"WE'D BETTER spread out!" Tom said in a hoarse whisper, as he and Jack Murray plunged in among the trees after the mysterious intruder. "He may try to zigzag and throw us off!"

"Right! But watch out for an ambush, skipper!" Jack called back.

The thick jungle growth made the search maddeningly difficult. Without machetes to cut their way through the tangled foliage, it was impossible to progress rapidly. Half a dozen times, Tom and Jack tripped over creepers or gnarled tree roots and nearly went sprawling.

The steamy gloom and stinging insects added to their misery. Both pursuers were soon dripping with perspiration.

"This is hopeless!" Tom realized, after beating the bush for twenty minutes. "Hey, Jack!

Where are you?" he called, cupping his hands.

The engineer finally rejoined him, and the two made their way back to the cave, where the others were waiting somewhat anxiously.

"Find anybody?" Chow asked.

"Not a trace, aside from that first quick glimpse," Tom replied, and whispered, "But at least we know now that Max's story was true."

From his fleeting glimpse of the mysterious man, Tom felt sure he was not a native. He had seemed too tall, and had light hair. Also, he was wearing a khaki shirt.

"Who do you suppose the fellow was?" Jack queried. "Some explorer doing field work?"

Tom shrugged. "It's a good guess. But if he *is* an explorer, he's behaving oddly."

"Some low-down jungle bushwhacker, that's who he is!" Chow declared firmly. "If I ever catch him snoopin' around, I'll rope an' hog-tie the critter!"

When they all met outside the cave, Tom asked Max if he would bring the carved bowl to the village. "I'd like to photograph it with a special camera to see how old it is. You could have it right back."

"Oh, you take it along," the giant said. "Those little men scare me, just like kids do."

The huge wrestler's admission seemed so incongruous that it was all Tom and his friends could do to refrain from laughing at him. Apparently Magnificent Max's boastfulness was more of a cover-up than they had suspected!

The young inventor smiled and said politely, "Thanks a lot. I'll see that the bowl is returned safely."

The four companions waved good-by and trudged back to the trail where the truck and jeep were parked.

"You want to drive the truck, Tom?" Chow asked.

Tom considered, then shook his head. "No, you and Jack take the truck and go on ahead," he decided. "I'll ride the jeep with Frenchy and carry the bowl in my hands."

"Okey-dokey. Drive careful, buckaroos!"

Jack took the wheel, Chow climbed into the cab beside him, and the truck rumbled off. Tom and Frenchy followed.

For a while both vehicles went slowly. Then, as the truck gradually increased speed, Frenchy also put on power in order to keep the truck in view. A few moments later the jeep's right wheel suddenly struck an unseen obstacle. The jolt threw Tom half off the seat and the precious bowl flew from his lap!

"Oh!" he exclaimed, making a desperate lunge out of the car. He grabbed the bowl in mid-air only a moment before it would have crashed to the ground!

"Nice catch, *mon ami!*" Frenchy commented with a smile.

Tom grinned wanly and clutched the bowl tighter than ever for the rest of the trip.

Bud Barclay and Dick Folsom hailed the travelers eagerly as they pulled into the village. "Did you lick that radiation problem, skipper?" Dick asked.

"I hope so." Tom showed the others his two compact little transmitter-radiator units and explained how they would operate in connection with the computer to screen out radiation from outside sources. "We'll try them out on this bowl," he added. "I have a hunch it contains space symbols."

Before the young inventor set to work on his experiment, Chow prepared a quick but tasty lunch of canned ham and tortillas. As the group ate, Tom related his exciting brush with the jaguar.

"Don't tell me you let Magnificent Max take away your trophy!" Bud joked. "Just think—you could have taken the hide back to Shopton! Or posed for a picture with your foot on the jaguar's head and labeled it 'Tom Swift, Lord of the Jungle!'"

Tom chuckled, then asked, "By the way, did any of you fellows take some practice shots with that rifle?"

The others shook their heads. "Funny thing,"

Tom remarked. "I was positive the rifle was fully loaded. Guess I must be getting absent-minded."

"Better watch it, professor," Bud advised. "That kind of absent-mindedness can get a guy in trouble!"

As soon as lunch was over, Tom hurried to the new hut to install the two field transmitters on his retroscope. The chief and several other natives watched with great curosity as Tom trained his camera on the Mayan bowl. An air of tense excitement filled the hut. What sort of carvings would be revealed on the bowl? Even more important, would Tom's new radiation-screening devices prove successful?

"Keep your fingers crossed," Tom muttered. He reset the computer so as to cancel out the disturbing radiation, then switched on power and made a number of hasty dial adjustments. The equipment hummed as the detectors began feeding a steady flow of electrical impulses to the camera's "brain."

"Hey, it's working like a charm!" Bud cried out. "And those *are* space symbols showing up!" A clear set was appearing on the screen of the reproducer unit, accompanied by the usual elaborate Mayan art designs.

"Nice going, skipper!" Jack Murray congratulated the young inventor.

Tom smiled with quiet satisfaction, but said

nothing until he had pulled the photographic film from the unit and studied it closely.

"It's the same message that appears on your sacred stone," he told Quetzal.

The chief stared at the pictures with a look of awe. "Some day, perhaps, we will learn more about my people's ancestors from the sky," he said hopefully.

Tom used his retroscope on a few more carvings on stones which the natives had brought to him. But he found no further mathematical space symbols. Finally he broke off his experiments.

"I sure wish we could start digging," he told Bud.

"Meaning you wish Señor Barancos from the Yucatan Institute would get here," Bud replied.

"Right. And, Bud, I have some good news for you. We have visitors coming tomorrow—Sandy, Phyl, and my dad!"

Bud was thrilled at the announcement and Chow immediately made plans for a second feast. Ahau Quetzal and his villagers also promised to take part in the celebration. The white-clad Mayan women were especially excited at the prospect of seeing two *señoritas* from the United States.

"In the meantime, I want to get the paraplane ready," said Tom. He radioed orders to the *Sky Queen* to bring fuel for it at once. Then he and Bud drove off in the jeep to drain the ship's tanks of the water seepage and supervise the refueling operation.

Within minutes the huge three-decker craft was hovering over the treetops above the paraplane. A hose was payed out and connected to the grounded ship. In a short time a fresh supply of fuel was pumped into the plane's tanks.

"All set!" Tom signaled after the two boys had disconnected the hose. It was reeled in and the Flying Lab soared off toward its own landing spot. Tired but full of anticipation, Tom and Bud drove back to the village.

"Boy, I can hardly wait to see Sandy!" Bud declared. Reddening slightly, he added, "I mean Phyl too, of course, and your dad."

Tom grinned. "You and me both, pal!"

The next morning the whole village turned out to greet the visitors from Shopton. Excited native runners had already brought news of their approach. Mr. Swift was driving a jeep, with the two girls seated beside him in gay summer dresses and large-brimmed straw hats.

"Hi, Dad!" Tom exclaimed as they shook hands. "Glad you found the landing spot okay."

"No trouble at all," the elder Swift replied, smiling. "I expected a bit of a drive from your jungle airport, so we brought along another jeep."

There was a strong resemblance between the famous scientist and his son. Both had the same

keen, deep-set blue eyes, although Tom was taller
and rangier than his father.

The native children presented the two visiting
girls with beautiful bouquets of colorful jungle
blooms. Sandy, her eyes dancing, made a warm
speech of thanks in her high-school Spanish. The
Mayas applauded loudly.

"You next!" Tom said teasingly, turning to
Phyl.

Dark-haired and laughing as usual, Phyllis Newton shook her head. "Have to beg off, I'm afraid.
As you know, I'm studying French, but Dad in-
sists that I take Spanish next year."

Bud, in high spirits, was chatting and joking
with Sandy when Wilson Hutchcraft pushed his
way forward. "May I be introduced?" the Bostonian asked suavely, a bland smile on his face.

Bud gave the man a dark look, but performed
the introductions. Then, before Hutchcraft could
intrude further, Bud seized Sandy's arm. "Come
on. I'll show you the Grand Hotel they built for
us!" he announced.

Soon the aroma of native cookery filled the air
as Chow and the Mayan women prepared an elaborate feast. Again tables were laid in the open air in
the village plaza. All took their places.

"O-oh, good grief!" Sandy giggled as heaping
platters of food were brought out. "We'll have to
go on a diet, Phyl, as soon as we get home."

"Who cares!" Phyl retorted, sampling the

stewed chicken and molé sauce. "Chow, this is simply delicious!"

"Jest a little dish I whipped up." Chow beamed.

Suddenly there was a loud commotion and the sound of angry cries. To Tom's surprise, he saw Magnificent Max pushing his way among the feasters, looking wild-eyed and upset.

"Jeepers, who's that?" said Sandy, staring in awe as the enraged jungle giant strode straight toward their table.

"A friend of ours—at least he was yesterday," Tom whispered. Getting to his feet, Tom faced the ex-wrestler calmly, hoping to quiet him. "You're just in time to join us, Max," he said pleasantly. "We have some visitors who flew down from the States. This is my sister, Sandy—and Phyllis Newton—and my father, Mr. Swift."

"Mr. Swift, eh?" Max glared at the scientist, and thrust out his lower jaw belligerently. "Well, I'm sorry to tell you this, but I'm fighting mad! Your son's nothing but a low-down thief—and I've got proof!"

CHAPTER XV

SIGHTSEER OVERBOARD!

"MY BROTHER a thief!" Sandy Swift burst out indignantly. "You must be out of your mind!"

Tom said evenly, "I'm sure there's some mistake, but we'll straighten it out."

Before he could continue, Mr. Swift interposed. "That's a serious charge," he told Max in a calm, reasonable voice. "Suppose you tell us what happened."

"Your son sneaked into my cave and swiped some of my Mayan relics—that's what happened!" Max stormed.

Tom said icily, "You said you had proof. What proof?"

"Who else could have done it?" the giant insisted furiously. "You and your pals are the only ones who knew about 'em—and what's more you were mighty interested in 'em."

Glaring at Tom, Max shook his huge fist in the youth's face. "Go on—admit it!" he bellowed.

"You sneaked into my cave this morning while I was out picking nuts and guavas for my breakfast."

"I haven't been out of this village all morning," Tom said coldly. "If you'll just sit down and stop shouting, we can talk this over sensibly."

"Don't gimme that soft soap!" Max threatened. "I know you snitched those treasures! Either hand 'em over or I'll tear you limb from limb!"

The two girls were thoroughly frightened by now, and Frenchy hastily got up to lend a strong arm, but Tom waved him aside.

"The same way you killed that jaguar with your bare hands?" Tom asked the giant, with a twinkle in his eyes.

The question seemed to deflate Magnificent Max's blustering ego. "Okay, so you saved my life," the long-haired giant admitted sulkily. "But don't think that changes anything!"

"I believe I can convince you," Tom said gently. "Come with me."

He led the giant to the Swift hut and showed him the Mayan bowl, which had been carefully stored in a box lined with soft jungle grasses. "As you can see, the only thing of yours here is this bowl you lent us. Search the place yourself, if you don't believe me."

Max poked about halfheartedly, then turned back to Tom. "How do I know you don't have the stuff hidden somewhere else?" he grumbled.

Tom shrugged and handed him the bowl. "Since you don't trust me, take the bowl along, although it may be safer here, with the thief still at large. That goes for your other treasures, too."

Max blushed and fingered the bowl awkwardly, as if uncertain what to do with it. "Okay, maybe I was shooting off my mouth out of turn," he admitted. "You keep it."

He handed the bowl to Tom and the two returned to the village plaza. Mr. Swift and the others noted with relief that the giant's belligerence was gone; he actually looked shamefaced.

"Just forget what I said about your son, eh pal?" Max told the elder Swift. He added with a puzzled look on his broad pug face, "But I still can't figure out what happened to the stuff. If none of you guys took the treasures, who did?"

"Mebbe that skinny hombre is the thief," Chow piped up. "Ever think o' *him?*"

Max's jaw dropped open in a look of surprised consternation. "Hey! Maybe you got something there, old-timer! I better get back and hide the rest of my treasures before that skinny sneak pulls another fast one!"

"It might be a good idea," Tom agreed.

The giant lumbered off, pausing only long enough to call back over his shoulder, "Or maybe I'll bring 'em here for *you* to keep, Junior!"

As Max disappeared, Sandy gave a shudder. "Goodness! Where did that character come from?"

Tom described the ex-wrestler's background, explaining that he had come to Yucatan to recover from a long illness and then stayed on as a jungle hermit. "He's not a bad guy, really," Tom added with a chuckle. "Just a bit mixed up. Bud calls him Magnificent Max."

"Well, I think you were magnificent, the way you stood up to him!" Phyl declared. "He scared the wits out of me. I thought he was the missing link or something!"

Tom blushed at the admiring look in the girl's brown eyes and said quickly, "Underneath, Max is scared of his own shadow. I was pretty sure he wouldn't become violent."

Hutchcraft had observed the scene with malicious amusement when the giant had first appeared. But Chow's mention of a "skinny hombre" had brought a quick gleam of interest to his eyes. "Who is this skinny fellow you were talking about?" he asked the cook.

Chow grunted noncommittally. "Some sneakin' coyote what's been spyin' on us an' tryin' to make trouble," he replied.

Bud blurted out, "By the way, Hutch, where *were* you yesterday?"

The Bostonian's face turned splotchy red. "I was doing field work, if it's any of your business," he retorted. "And what's more, I don't like your insinuations!"

Mr. Swift hastily changed the subject. "This

cooking of yours is really a triumph, Chow!" he said. "Are you going to take back some of these recipes to Shopton?"

"I sure am!" The Westerner jumped up enthusiastically. "Say, that reminds me—we ain't had dessert yet!"

The last course consisted of a mouth-watering assortment of native fruits and nuts, including guavas, wild plums, oranges, plantains, and cashews. When everyone had finished eating, the Mayan musicians struck up another of their lively tunes, and the natives performed a gay dance.

"Wonderful!" Sandy said, applauding when the dance was over. "I wish we could have them play at the Shopton Country Club some time— they'd be a sensation!"

"The Rhythm Kings from Yucatan!" Bud laughed. "How about a tour of the village?"

The girls agreed eagerly, so Tom and Bud escorted them from the plaza. Mr. Swift, always a keen student of native cultures, lingered behind to chat with Ahau Quetzal. This gave Hutchcraft, who had shown a decided interest in Sandy, a chance to excuse himself and join the young people.

"I hear you're interested in Mayan dialects," Sandy said politely. Noticing Bud's quick scowl, she was anxious to start a conversation before another clash occurred.

"Yes, indeed," Hutchcraft said, putting on his

usual smile of superiority. "The Mayan tongue is a fascinating problem."

"A problem?" Sandy raised her eyebrows. "How so?"

"Well, no doubt in school you learned how Latin gradually died out and changed into other languages, such as Italian, French, and Spanish. It's the same way with ancient Mayan. Today it survives in the form of various dialects, but we don't really know what the old language was like."

"Don't tell me it's got even *you* baffled!" Bud needled.

"Oh, we linguists have deduced certain facts," Hutchcraft, unruffled, replied smoothly. "For instance, we believe that the language spoken down in the Guatemalan highlands and up in the northern part of Yucatan belongs to the same branch— called Yucatec."

"Didn't the language change a lot when the Mayas were invaded by warlike tribes, especially the Toltecs?" Tom put in.

Hutchcraft nodded. "The invaders spoke a language called nahuatl. They added many words to the Mayan tongue, although the form and grammar of the old language probably remained pretty much the same."

By this time, the strollers had reached the outskirts of the village. A little way beyond, Phyl noticed a huge, deep-sided pool with white limestone walls.

"My goodness, what's that?" she exclaimed. "Not a swimming pool, surely!"

"It's the village well," Bud told her.

"Actually, it's called a *cenote*," Hutchcraft corrected him. "You see, Yucatan is a parched country, in spite of all this tropical vegetation. There are no lakes or rivers. The only water is the rain which soaks below the surface and is held in the limestone rock. The wells occur at points where the limestone crust has caved in. The Mayas usually build their villages close to a cenote so as to have a water supply."

As the group strolled closer to peer into the well, Bud muttered to Tom, "Listen to that guy spout off—he knows it all! I'll bet he just boned up on this stuff to impress Sandy!"

Tom grinned but said nothing, lest Hutchcraft overhear them.

The well was as large as a good-sized pond. Its water, cool, sparkling, and deep, lay about ten feet below ground surface. Hutchcraft, who obviously enjoyed showing off his knowledge, continued his lecture.

"At the ancient Mayan capital of Chichen Itza, there are two cenotes," he said. "One was used for human sacrifice. But this was due to the influence of the Toltecs."

The girls were horrified. "You mean they *drowned* people in them?" Sandy exclaimed.

Hutchcraft nodded. "As a gesture to their rain

god, beautiful maidens who were going to be married were shoved in. They were so weighted with heavy jewelry that they invariably sank at once. Sometimes the grooms-to-be jumped in too. What say we re-enact the custom and get cooled off?"

"No thanks!" said Sandy.

Hutchcraft advanced on her jokingly, as if to carry out his playful suggestion. Sandy backed away hastily. But as she dodged his outstretched hand, she lost her balance, gave a scream of fright, and toppled into the well!

Bud was furious. "You dope!" he cried out at Hutchcraft. "Maybe you'd like to get dunked yourself!"

The Bostonian gulped and turned pale as he saw that Bud meant business. "No, no! I can't swim!" he pleaded. Ducking away from the outraged Bud, Hutchcraft fled toward the village in panic.

Meanwhile, Tom and Phyl were anxiously watching for Sandy to appear.

"Something's wrong!" Phyl cried in alarm.

Tom was about to dive in when Bud said, "I'll go." He did not wait even to remove his heavy hiking boots.

The others waited tensely and gave sighs of relief as Sandy and Bud rose to the surface together. They swam to the edge and clambered up the steep side.

Sandy toppled into the well

"You scared us silly, Sandy," Phyl said as her friend reached the top. "What happened?"

Sandy laughed. "I thought as long as I'd played being a sacrificed maiden, I'd see if I could pick up some ancient jewelry in the well." She made a wry face. "Nothing on the bottom but mud!"

The blazing tropical sun, almost directly overhead, soon dried the swimmers' clothing. When the four young people finally returned to the village, they found that Hutchcraft had "gone for a walk."

"Smart move!" Tom commented with a chuckle. "He didn't like that fighting gleam in your eye, Bud!" Turning to Phyllis Newton, the young inventor added, "How would you like to take a trip with me in my new paraplane? We can fly over to the *Sky Queen*—if my crate will start, that is."

"I'd love to!" Phyl said.

As she and Tom climbed into one jeep, Sandy and Bud got into the other, saying they were going on a little exploring expedition of their own.

When Tom and Phyl reached the paraplane, the young inventor made a quick check of the ship. Then he and Phyl climbed into the flight cabin.

"So far, so good," Tom remarked, after warming up the jet engine. Then he switched on the pump and waited for the dirigible bag to fill with helium. "Now we'll see what happens," he said, a tinge of worry in his voice.

CHAPTER XVI

POLICE QUIZ

"IS SOMETHING wrong, Tom?" Phyl asked in bewilderment. She had expected the paraplane to take off immediately.

"Look up there." Tom grinned in relief and pointed to the transparent panel overhead.

Phyl gasped as she saw the dirigible bag slowly billow out to its full shape. The plane began to rise as she watched. "Oh, Tom! This is super!" she said excitedly.

The young pilot jockeyed the ship gently with rudder and elevators to keep it on a straight upward course. Presently the plane cleared the treetops.

"What a thrill!" Phyl exclaimed. "It's like floating on air!"

Tom pressed a button on the control panel, and

the paraplane's wings swung outward from the fuselage. "Speaking of floating," he said, "how'd you like to 'float' over to the Flying Lab?"

"You mean, without using the jet—just as if we were in a balloon?" Phyl asked.

Tom nodded, smiling. "More or less. There's a pretty fair wind up here, and it's blowing in the right direction. I believe I can steer us there just using the rudder and other controls."

"Then let's!" Phyl agreed gaily. "This is fun!"

By now, they had gained enough altitude so that the jungle lay spread out below them in a lush green expanse. Tom banked and circled until the ship was headed on a course which would take them straight toward the spot where the *Sky Queen* and Mr. Swift's cargo jet were berthed. Then he cut the engines completely.

"Now I can understand why people become so enthusiastic about gliders!" Phyl said excitedly. "I feel just like a bird up here!"

Tom switched on the radio to make contact with the *Sky Queen*. Its radioman responded immediately to the call.

"Phyl and I are headed your way in the paraplane," Tom reported. "We're doing a free-balloon stunt, so it may take us a while to get there."

"Good thing you raised us, skipper," the radioman replied. "We just had a call from Shopton for your dad and we haven't been able to reach him at the village. He's wanted in Washington as soon as possible for government conferences on a new space project. Can you give him the message?"

"Sure thing," Tom promised. "If I can't get through on the radio, we'll go back and tell him in person."

Fortunately, Bud had turned on the radio in the jeep he was driving. He said that he and Sandy would return to camp immediately and relay the message to Tom's father. Within minutes, Mr. Swift's voice came over the air.

"I'm afraid this means that the girls and I will have to fly home at once, son," the scientist said. "Sorry our trip has to be cut short before we've seen your retroscope in action."

"I wish you could stick around, Dad," Tom said regretfully, "but I realize your government work is more important. Would you like us to turn around and pick you and Sandy up?"

Mr. Swift chuckled. "No, don't bother. Bud tells me you're trying a bit of lighter-than-air navigation, so go ahead with your experiment. Sandy and I probably will beat you there in the jeep."

"Don't count on that!" Tom said, and signed off with a laugh.

Presently Phyl, using binoculars, sighted the jeep threading its way along the jungle trail below. "This race may turn out to be neck-and-neck!" she reported.

"Don't sell us short," Tom joked. "The future of the airship is at stake!"

After almost an hour of free-floating, the landing site finally came into view. Below, in the broad grassy clearing, lay the huge silver-winged *Sky Queen* and Mr. Swift's smaller cargo jet. Tom hovered down over the clearing, switched on the electric pump and compressor to deflate the helium bag, and landed without difficulty.

The jeep—Phyl had reported from her last view through the binoculars—was a mile or so away. "Winner and still champion!" She laughed, raising Tom's hand. "Seriously, Tom, I think your paraplane is wonderful!"

The young inventor reddened and laughed. "It was fun, especially with you, Phyl. How about an airship picnic when we get back to Shopton?"

"It's a date!" Phyl said enthusiastically.

Mr. Swift and Sandy arrived soon afterward. The girls were disappointed at having their visit cut short, but cheered up when Tom promised an outing and a full report of all adventures as soon as he and Bud returned home from Yucatan.

"And remember—no excuses about being too busy," Sandy warned. "While you're at it, you might bring us back some antique Mayan jewelry."

"That's against the law, Sis," Tom replied with a chuckle. "But I might manage an old stone carving."

"I couldn't wear that!" Sandy pretended to pout.

"Good luck, son," Mr. Swift said, shaking hands. "I'll be interested in hearing your report myself, especially if you run down any more clues on that mysterious space armada."

"Right, Dad. I'll keep you posted."

After a final farewell, Mr. Swift and the girls boarded the cargo jet and took off. Tom waved as the plane dipped its wings and streaked northward into the blue.

The young inventor then walked to the *Sky Queen*. He had several ideas for improvements on his restroscope that he wished to work on before returning to camp. He had hardly seated himself in his private laboratory aboard the huge ship when Doc Simpson burst in excitedly.

"There's a helicopter overhead, skipper," the medic reported. "I think it's going to land!"

Tom rushed out to see for himself. The big twin-rotored transport was slowly descending toward the clearing.

"That's no private whirlybird," a crewman remarked, squinting his eyes.

"It's a Mexican government ship," Tom replied, after studying its markings through binoculars.

In a few moments the helicopter touched down. Three men climbed out, wearing khaki police uniforms. Two of the men carried carbines. The third, tall and swarthy, was evidently an officer. He came forward and saluted briskly.

"May I ask who is in charge here, *señores?*" he inquired in English.

"I am," Tom replied. "My name is Tom Swift Jr. and these men are all members of my expedition. We're from the United States."

"I am Jefe Luis Rodriguez of the Yucatan State Policia," the police chief said in a coldly official tone. "Your papers, please."

Tom handed over the documents. The *jefe* scrutinized these for a moment, then said, "Native gossip has it that a group of Americans are disturbing the valuable Mayan ruins in these parts. Are you the ones?"

"I've examined some relics, if that's what you mean," Tom admitted. "You see, I've invented a new type of camera which reveals the original carvings on stone and also the age of any inscription. However, we haven't begun digging yet, although we intend to."

"By whose permission?" Rodriguez snapped in an unfriendly manner.

Tom, who was accustomed to pleasant, courteous treatment from the Mexican authorities, was amazed. "Our trip was arranged through the University of Mexico and your *aduana,* as you can see from our identification papers," Tom explained.

"These papers state merely that you are to fly several Mayas back to your country for a medical research project," Rodriguez said. "They do not mention any archaeological work."

"I'm sorry. I should have made that clear," Tom said politely. "The Mayas have already been flown to the United States. Permission to excavate the local ruins was arranged after we arrived here. Señor Marco Barancos of the Institute of Anthropology and History in Yucatan is coming to supervise our work."

The swarthy police chief frowned and exchanged several remarks in Spanish with the other two policemen, whom he addressed as Pedro and Miguel. Then he turned back to Tom.

"I am afraid, señor, that without proof, your story is unconvincing," he said bluntly. "Where is this Señor Barancos you speak of?"

Tom shrugged. "Frankly, I don't know. I've been wondering myself why he hasn't arrived."

"Very strange, is it not?" said Rodriguez sarcastically. "We have only your word that this man Barancos even exists."

The young inventor flushed angrily at the police chief's tone. He struggled to keep his temper. At that moment Doc Simpson put in hastily, "This officer may have a point, skipper. It does seem funny that Barancos hasn't shown up."

"I'm sure there's nothing wrong," Tom insisted firmly. "My father made the arrangements through the same authorities who okayed the medical project."

Rodriguez mulled this over somewhat suspiciously. Pedro and Miguel, who seemed to have followed the conversation in English, spoke to him in an undertone.

After a whispered conference, Rodriguez said, "Very well, señores, we will take no action for the moment. However, we wish to inspect this new camera you spoke of."

Tom explained that his camera equipment was at Ahau Quetzal's village, about ten miles away. "I'm afraid there's no clearing there big enough for your transport to land," he added. "If you like, I can give you a lift." Tom gestured toward his paraplane.

The three officers stared in astonishment at the strange-looking craft. "What sort of an airplane is that, señor?" the police chief demanded.

"When the wings are extended, it flies as a conventional jet," Tom explained. "There's also a dirigible bag enclosed in the dome on top of the fuselage, which can be used for take-off or landing in tight spots. I've already landed it near the village."

The three members of the policia scowled and scratched their jaws uneasily. It was evident that they were none too eager to board such a weird-looking aircraft. But realizing that it was a choice between taking the paraplane or hiking ten miles through the jungle, Pedro and Miguel shrugged helplessly.

"We accept your offer—*gracias*," Rodriguez announced at last.

Tom warmed up the paraplane and gave the three officers a hand as they climbed aboard. Then he flicked the control switch to fill the bag with helium. The ship rose gently from the clearing.

"*Caramba!*" the police chief muttered as they floated above the treetops. "Most remarkable!"

Tom extended the wings and opened the throttle slightly. The ship speared gracefully toward the Mayan village. But suddenly Tom realized that the rudder and elevators were not responding properly.

Alarmed, he worked the stick and control pedals. Again, only a feeble response! With a sinking feeling Tom knew that he and his passengers were scudding helplessly over an unbroken expanse of forest, with no possible spot for an emergency landing!

CHAPTER XVII

THE BURIED TEMPLE

TOM shot a quick glance at Luis Rodriguez. The police chief was staring down at the jungle scenery, while Pedro and Miguel talked volubly in Spanish. Apparently none of them realized yet that the paraplane was crippled.

"I won't alarm these men yet," Tom decided. "Maybe I can figure out some plan of action."

Sweating under the tension, the young inventor cut throttle and sized up the situation. His indicator dial showed that the wind direction had changed sharply. It was now blowing inland from the sea—away from both the village and the *Sky Queen's* clearing.

"Not a chance of gliding to safety," Tom told himself grimly. "I'd better think fast!"

Suddenly an idea occurred to him. A skillful sailor, Tom had often tacked a sailboat upwind on Lake Carlopa. "Perhaps," he thought, "by inflating and deflating the dirigible bag, I can tack vertically against the wind in the paraplane! It's worth a try. But first I'll have to get this crate aimed on course!"

There was barely enough response left in the controls to enable Tom to bank the craft slightly. By gunning the jet in quick spurts, he was able to maneuver the ship about, so that it was headed back toward the clearing.

Rodriguez threw Tom a puzzled glance. "We are turning back?"

Tom nodded curtly, hoping to avoid further explanation. The police chief scowled suspiciously, but said nothing.

Tom switched on the helium pump full power. As the dirigible bag swelled to its greatest size, the plane shot upward. Then Tom deflated the bag and used his increased altitude to coast downward into the wind. This brought the ship considerably closer to the clearing. Again Tom ballooned the ship upward, then repeated the same tactic.

Rodriguez burst out angrily, "What is this, señor—a trick of some kind? I demand an explanation at once!"

"Something has happened to the controls. This is the only way I can get back to the clearing."

After further maneuvering, Tom brought the ship down. Doc Simpson and the crewmen from the Flying Lab came rushing up.

"The controls are dead," Tom said tersely as he

and his passengers climbed out. "I think something has happened to the hydraulic system."

"And *I* think you have done this on purpose!" Rodriguez growled suspiciously. "Why? Because you do not wish us to see what you have been doing at the Mayan village!"

"Think what you please," Tom retorted, out of patience. "We're lucky we didn't crack up."

Unscrewing the cowl panels, he made a quick check of the paraplane's hydraulic system. "There's the answer." He pointed to a hose from the main pump. The hose had a leak through which the hydraulic fluid had oozed out, causing a loss of operating pressure.

"Well, I'll be doggoned!" Stu Kern, the *Sky Queen's* flight engineer, scratched his head. "For a new ship, that hose sure didn't last long!"

"Maybe the rubber rotted in this jungle atmosphere," another crewman conjectured.

"That hose isn't made of rubber," Stu pointed out. "It's a synthetic plastic that's impervious to heat or humidity. The hose section must have been faulty to begin with. But it's hard to believe the inspectors at Swift Construction slipped up and let that go by!"

The Swift Construction Company, managed by Phyl Newton's father, built the production models of all inventions developed by Swift Enterprises. Knowing the company's rigid standards of inspection, Tom agreed with Stu.

"There's another possibility," he said grimly. "It could be sabotage."

Tom's remark shocked his listeners. "You mean somebody slit the hose on purpose—just since we've arrived here?" Doc exclaimed. "But why?"

Tom shrugged. "Wish I knew the answer. Someone seems to have it in for us." He related how the ship's helium tanks had been emptied.

Realizing that the youth was in earnest, Chief Rodriguez demanded, "If there is a criminal at large, why did you not tell me, señor?"

"I had no definite evidence," Tom replied. "In fact, I still haven't. Even this hose leak *could* have been an accident."

"If you'd crashed, it would have been murder!" Doc Simpson declared angrily.

Tom frowned. "Somehow I don't think our enemy—if we have one—is trying to get rid of us," he mused. "All he accomplished by opening the helium cocks was to ground the plane. Same with this hydraulic leak, only I took the ship up too soon."

Stu Kern replaced the leaky hose and refilled the hydraulic system. He also insisted that every inch of the paraplane be checked. Police Chief Rodriguez and his two constables, still suspicious, fumed at this new delay.

Suddenly the noise of a car engine was heard through the trees. Moments later, a jeep pulled into the clearing with a Mayan driver at the wheel.

Beside him sat a plump, olive-skinned man with a black mustache. He was wearing shorts and a sun helmet, and clutched a brief case in one hand.

Climbing out, he looked at the group questioningly. "Señor Tom Swift?"

The young inventor stepped forward, and the fat man shook hands. "I am Señor Marco Barancos of the Institute of Anthropology and History of Yucatan," he announced.

"I'm certainly glad to meet you." Tom smiled. "We've been expecting you for some time."

Señor Barancos nodded wearily. "Sí, señor, I must apologize for the delay but I was busy at another exploration site." Taking off his sun helmet, he mopped his forehead. "What a bad time we had getting here! In places this jungle is almost impassable."

Rodriguez bustled up to quiz the visitor. "So you are Barancos, eh?" he said officiously. "May I see your papers please, señor?"

Barancos opened his brief case and produced several documents. "Here you are. As you can see, the Institute has granted Señor Swift permission to excavate, and these are my official orders to assist him!"

Rodriguez scanned the papers with a scowl. "It appears that everything is in order. Since you have a jeep, my men and I will ride with you to the village where the digging is to take place. *Vamonos!* Let us go!"

Barancos flicked his mustache. "We will leave when I am ready and no sooner," he stated flatly. "My driver and I are very tired. First we must rest and have something to eat."

Tom and his friends suppressed grins. Evidently Señor Barancos was not a man to be bullied. "You can relax and have a shower aboard our plane if you like," Tom offered, gesturing toward the *Sky Queen*.

The archaeologist and his driver gratefully accepted. Both were amazed when they saw the comfortable lounge, sleeping quarters, and galley of the huge three-decker ship.

Later that afternoon, greatly refreshed, Barancos announced he was ready to leave. Tom and his crew were still busy overhauling the paraplane. They waved as the jeep pulled away, loaded with its five passengers.

Within an hour Tom was ready to take off. Doc Simpson, eager to see the Mayan village, went aboard with him. They landed in the plane's former "jungle hangar," then hiked the rest of the way to the village. Twilight was falling by the time they entered it.

Bud, Chow, and the others in Tom Swift's party greeted them eagerly. "What's with these Mexican cops?" Bud inquired. "Don't they trust us?"

"Not completely, I'm afraid," Tom replied. "But Señor Barancos is on our side, so I think everything will be okay."

Chow prepared a hearty supper, which seemed to mellow Police Chief Rodriguez considerably. After a final conference with Señor Barancos, Rodriguez agreed to permit Tom to dig for Mayan relics in the area around the village.

"But you must work only with trowels," the archaeologist warned. "I cannot risk having any valuable Mayan art objects damaged by a pick or shovel."

"Okay, that's understood," Tom agreed.

The next morning he asked the villagers to check on the paraplane once in a while to see if it was all right. Then he and Bud stepped up into the truck, with the retroscope equipment loaded aboard. Ahau Quetzal asked to ride with them. "I can show you places to dig!" he promised.

"Fine!" Tom said.

Marco Barancos and the three policemen followed in the archaeologist's jeep. Doc Simpson and the two Swift engineers brought up the rear, riding the jeep from the *Sky Queen*.

Quetzal pointed out several spots in the forest mentioned in village folklore as the sites of buried relics. At each location Tom made a test probe beneath the surface, using the detector circuits of his camera in a hookup with the Swift spectroscope. The most promising site proved to be a huge mound, overgrown with jungle vegetation. Here, the spectroscope analysis showed underground stone deposits which might be Mayan ruins.

"We've got to dig all this up with hand trowels?" Bud asked.

"Sí, until you find what lies below," Barancos replied. "Then, perhaps, it will be safe to use shovels in exploring further."

The archaeologist marked out a small area for test-digging near the top of the mound, then Tom and Bud set to work.

Meanwhile, Chow had finished his breakfast chores back in the village and set out to join the party. The old cook slung a pick over one shoulder, not knowing of Señor Barancos' ruling.

"Shucks, they'll never get nowhere with them teeny li'l trowels," Chow muttered as he caught sight of Tom and Bud working on top of the mound. "I reckon an ole range hand like me kin show 'em how to swing a pick!"

At that moment Tom gave a shout. "I think we've found something!"

Señor Barancos and the others rushed up to see. The boys had uncovered some flat stone slabs. "What do you suppose they are?" Bud asked.

"Perhaps a stone platform for religious ceremonies," Barancos replied. "Or it may be the roof of a building. Señores, the old Mayan architects never learned to construct an arch with a keystone but used a flat capstone. That is why most of their buildings were flat-roofed.

"If the structure has crumbled, it may be somewhat shaky," he cautioned. "Proceed carefully with your digging. The rest of us had better leave the mound."

Chow was so intent on his own digging that he had heard none of this conversation. In the excitement, no one had noticed the Texan, who was partly hidden by the jungle foliage. Suddenly he gave a mighty heave with his pick. There was a rumbling noise underground, followed by yells of alarm from Tom and Bud. With a shattering clatter of stone and debris, the center of the mound caved in!

"Great snakes!" Chow gulped, aghast at the havoc he had caused.

Both boys had disappeared from view!

The cook scrambled up to the edge of the cave-in, with Barancos and the others at his heels. They peered down into the gaping hole, but it was too dark to make out what had happened to the boys.

"Hey, fellers!" Chow called down in a quavering voice. "You okay?"

He heaved a gusty sigh of relief as Tom's voice came back, "Sure—just shaken up. But send down a light. I think we're in some kind of a room— maybe a temple."

Dick Folsom hurried to the truck for a battery-powered lantern. It was lowered into the hole on a rope.

"Got it—thanks!" Tom shouted up.

The center of the mound caved in!

A moment later the yellow glow of the lantern illumined the underground chamber.

"It's a tomb!" Bud exclaimed.

The stone-walled room was lined with skeletons, propped in sitting position! None seemed over four feet tall. Necklaces of jade beads hung around their necks. On one wall was carved the figure of Kukulcan. Near the skeletons stood bowls and other items of pottery.

"What a find!" Bud muttered.

Suddenly Tom gave a fresh cry of excitement. "Bud! Look!"

The copilot turned. Tom was pointing to a series of strange markings carved on one wall of the tomb.

"More space symbols!" he exclaimed.

CHAPTER XVIII

SABOTAGE

"CAN YOU translate these space symbols, Tom?" Bud asked eagerly, staring at the wall markings.

"Part of the message is the same as the inscription on the sacred stone and Max's bowl—*'Fifty of us flew in here without mishap. We will hunt for the rest of the armada.'* The other—"

Haltingly, Tom managed to decode a further portion of the message. It said: *"We hope to survive here but will have to get used to the strange food. Our own supply is nearly gone."*

"I'm afraid that's all I can dope out right now," Tom concluded, after puzzling over the symbols for several more minutes. "I'll need the space dictionary to figure out the rest."

"Boy, this may tell the whole story!" Bud exulted. "Have you got a copy of the dictionary in the truck?"

Tom shook his head. "No, I left it in the *Sky*

Queen. Bud, I must get the electronic retroscope down here and find out when these symbols were carved!"

"Are you kidding?" Bud stared at his friend. "You'll never get that big clunker down this hole."

"You're right," the young inventor agreed. "Which means I'll have to build a new one—completely miniaturized."

Bud whistled and shook his head. "You're a demon for work, pal, but more power to you! In the meantime, what do we do next?"

"Take some pictures of these relics."

Tom called up to the group above and asked that two pocket cameras, one for developing pictures on the spot, be brought from his luggage and lowered to him. This was soon done, and with Bud holding the lantern, he made several snaps of the relics, Kukulcan, and the symbols. The boys were then hauled to the surface. Señor Barancos and the others were astounded to learn of their valuable find and gazed at the pictures in awe. Quetzal was even more impressed when Tom told him as much of the additional message in the symbols as he could translate without the space dictionary.

"I will stay here and guard the treasures below with my life!" Quetzal promised.

"The police can do that," Tom said. "It will be better if you can get some of your people to help us excavate. There will be much to do for everyone in the village."

Quetzal eagerly agreed to recruit a number of his tribesmen to assist with the digging.

"What is your plan, Señor Swift?" Barancos inquired.

"I believe we should try to uncover the whole tomb," Tom replied. "It may be part of a larger building, such as a temple or palace."

"You are right," the expert nodded. "A priceless discovery such as this should be explored thoroughly! As soon as possible, we must try to map an outline of the structure!" His voice showed keen excitement.

Tom announced that he would return to the Flying Lab immediately to begin work on a smaller model of his electronic retroscope. He asked the two engineers, Dick Folsom and Jack Murray, to come with him and help on the job of miniaturization.

"Bud, I'd like you to stay here and keep an eye on things. Watch out especially for more space symbols when the digging gets underway. And take step-by-step pictures with your thirty-five-millimeter movie camera as the digging proceeds."

"Roger!"

After a quick farewell, Tom and the two engineers piled into the jeep and drove to the paraplane. Three smiling village men walked up and said in Spanish that they hoped the "sky bird" was all right.

"Was anyone here?" Tom asked.

"Just giant. We ran away for while, then come back."

Tom nodded and thought with amusement, as he and the engineers climbed into the para-plane, "They're afraid of Max and he's afraid of them!"

Before turning on the power, Tom flicked on the radio. "I'd better call the Flying Lab and get things rolling," he explained to his companions. "We'll need a stack of parts flown down from Shopton for the new retroscope."

After waiting several moments, Tom noticed that the set showed no sign of warming up. He whipped out a pocket screw driver and removed a panel so as to expose the chassis. None of the tubes were glowing!

"What's wrong?" Jack Murray asked from the rear seat.

"No power." Puzzled, Tom switched on the helium pump, then tried several other circuits. None gave the slightest response. Apparently the ship's whole electrical system was dead!

"You're using solar batteries in this job, aren't you?" Dick Folsom put in.

Tom nodded. "And they've never conked out before."

These small but powerful units were one of

Tom Swift's most successful inventions. They were charged by direct, unshielded rays from the sun on an assembly line in the Swifts' space station, high above the earth's atmosphere.

Worried and suspecting further sabotage, despite the guards, Tom quickly opened a small compartment just below the paraplane's control panel. Half a dozen solar batteries stood banked inside. Tom gave a cry of dismay. Every one of the batteries had swelled and cracked its catalium plastic case!

"Good night! What happened?" Jack gasped, crowding forward for a closer look.

"Good question," Tom replied grimly. On a hunch, he disconnected one of the batteries.

"Maybe the heat or humidity caused a chemical reaction," Dick suggested.

"Maybe—and then again maybe not." Tom sniffed the chemical compound that had leaked out of the cracked cylinder. "I intend to check this and make sure. In the meantime, it looks as if we'll have to use the jeep."

Urging the natives to keep closer tabs on the paraplane, the trio climbed into the jeep again and started off through the jungle, heading toward the *Sky Queen*. Halfway along the trail, they sighted Magnificent Max plodding toward them.

"Do you think he tampered with the plane while the guards were away?" Dick muttered.

"No, he isn't bright enough," Tom replied.

The giant seemed strangely gaunt and haggard. He was staggering under the weight of an enormous, crude knapsack slung over one shoulder.

Tom braked the jeep to a halt. "Hi, Max! What is this—moving day?"

Max dumped the bag on the ground and wiped the sweat off his face with a brawny forearm. "Hello! I sure am glad you came along, Junior. You're just the guy I wanted to see! Here, take this stuff, will you?" He hoisted the bag into the rear seat of the jeep.

"What is it?"

"My treasures," the ex-wrestler replied. "You keep 'em. Or give 'em to a museum or something'."

"How come?" Tom asked.

" 'Cause they're just too much to worry about, that's how come." Max slumped down wearily beside the jeep. "It's got so I can't sleep any more at night. All I do is stew and worry about someone swiping these things."

"Has someone tried?" Tom asked quickly. "I mean, since that first theft you told us about."

"No, but I have a hunch they're just waiting for the right chance," Max replied. "At night I hear noises outside the cave, like someone walking. It's not animals, either, 'cause I can't ever see any eyes glowing in the dark!"

"Any idea who the prowler might be?"

"That skinny guy, most likely," Max said. "The same sneak you fellows chased—who else?"

Turning to Tom, the giant added, "And that ain't all. You know what happened last night?"

The young inventor shook his head. "What?"

"Well, I couldn't sleep, so I figured I'd go get you and talk things over, see? You seem like a pretty smart cookie, so I thought between us, we could figure out some way to trap that dirty rat. Well, when I got near your plane, I saw a light inside!"

"A light!" Tom stared at the speaker with a worried frown. "What happened?"

"Nothing. When I got closer, the light went out. It was quite dark, so I couldn't see much, but then I heard footsteps. Well, I called out your name, thinking it might be you. But no one answered! All I could hear was somebody rushing off through the bushes!"

Tom exchanged troubled glances with his two companions. "Do you suppose that explains those ruined batteries, skipper?" asked Dick Folsom.

"Could be," Tom replied. "And it happened while the guards were away."

Max heaved himself wearily to his feet. "You guys figure it out. This whole business is driving me nuts! But take good care of those treasures now, y'hear?"

Tom nodded reassuringly. "Don't worry about them. Just take it easy and get some rest. I don't know what our skinny spy is up to, Max, but I have a hunch it's me he's after—not you."

Max brightened somewhat. "I sure hope so—not that I wish you guys any bad luck. Well, so long!" With a wave of his huge hand, the long-haired giant trudged off and soon disappeared from view among the trees.

Tom and his companions resumed their journey. When they reached the *Sky Queen,* Tom rushed to his laboratory immediately to test the damaged battery. He scraped off some of the spilled compound, then studied the mass under a Swift spectroscope.

"What's the answer?" Jack Murray asked.

Tom's face was grave. "It was sabotage, all right. Someone spiked our batteries with sulphuric acid!"

Switching on the intercom, Tom issued orders to Stu Kern and another crewman. "Hop in the jeep and drive to the village, pronto! Tell Bud I now have proof that the plane has been sabotaged and to keep *all* our equipment guarded, night and day! Tell him to watch out for that skinny guy—he may try to wreck my electronic retroscope!"

CHAPTER XIX

A STARTLING CONFESSION

AS SOON as the crewmen took off in the jeep, Tom sat down to a hasty conference with the two engineers. "Let's see if we can map out the general design of the new retroscope in a hurry," he told them.

Tom's pencil fairly flew over the paper as he sketched the various circuits. "I believe we can use the old brain and reproducer units—but above-ground," he decided. "We'll just run longer cables from the scanning rig, and change the input and output impedance."

"You mean you'll take only the camera down to the underground room?" Dick Folsom asked.

"Yes, and I'll divide that into two parts; the scanner and a cabinet to hold certain electronic components."

"You'll have to build your field transmitters into the camera housing," Jack spoke up.

"True," Tom agreed.

Dick Folsom came up with a suggestion. "Getting rid of all the tubes would cut the size of the camera."

"Right. We'll transistorize everything."

"And let's install smaller transformers," Jack Murray added. "Here, for example, the new X-24's should do it."

Tom nodded. "We'll start itemizing the stuff to send for."

With the list completed, Tom hurried topside to the radio compartment.

"Contact Shopton," he told the operator. "Give Dilling this list. Ask him to shoot them down here on a cargo jet as fast as possible."

Tom returned to the laboratory. This amazing compartment was divided into cubicles—each one equipped with the latest devices for research in specialized fields of science. Dick and Jack were already busy in the metalworking shop, turning out the chassis and housing for the new two-part camera.

"Nice going!" Tom said approvingly. "While you're doing that, I'll work on the detectors."

By midnight, after almost continuous work, the trio had completed as much of the new retroscope as could be assembled until the extra parts arrived. Shortly after daybreak the cargo jet from Shopton touched down in the clearing, and the awaited stock of parts was unloaded at once. After an early breakfast, Tom, Jack, and Dick plunged back to work. Soon the compact assembly began taking shape on the workbench.

"Boy, that camera chassis is crammed tighter than a can of sardines." Dick chuckled.

"It's a swell job of miniaturization—thanks to you fellows," Tom said approvingly.

Jack Murray flashed a pleased grin, but remarked, "Don't kid the experts. It's your design."

An hour later the truck pulled into the clearing with Stu Kern at the wheel. He boarded the *Sky Queen* and hurried up a steel-ribbed ladder to the young inventor's private laboratory.

"I have an urgent message from Bud," he said. Stu fished in his pocket and handed over a letter. It read:

Dear Tom:
Yesterday Barancos removed some things from the tomb and I decided to check them with the retroscope. It worked fine—till the brain unit short-circuited! Last night the police were supposed to guard the equipment, but Pedro and Miguel fell asleep. This morning I tried to fix the short circuit. Believe it or not, the brain unit was already repaired! . . . You figure it out!

Your befogged pal,
Bud

Tom showed the letter to Dick and Jack, who read it with puzzled grins. "This *is* crazy!" Dick remarked. "What do you make of it, skipper?"

"Beats me. Maybe the mysterious spy is also an electronics man. But what's his game?" Tom frowned thoughtfully. "Tell Bud I'll be back soon to help him, Stu."

By late afternoon the miniaturized camera was completed. Tom double-checked every circuit for possible errors in assembly. Then he set out for the village in the jeep with Jack and Dick. By the time they arrived, the native cook-fires were glowing in the dusk. Chow had prepared an appetizing meal, which everyone ate with a hearty appetite.

After supper Bud Barclay drew Tom aside. "I've been doing a little sleuthing, and I believe this guy Hutchcraft didn't come here just to study languages!"

"What!" Tom exclaimed in amazement.

"He's up to something else—something he hasn't told us about."

"What gives you that idea?"

"Tom, I saw him not far from where I was digging this afternoon. He hid a fat envelope under a big flat stone. Then he took out several tools and some wire."

Tom's eyes narrowed with interest. "Tools? What did he do with them?"

"There you've got me, pal," Bud answered.

"Just then Barancos called me, so I had to go. By the time I was through, Hutchcraft was gone."

Tom mulled this over. Should he question the man at once, or merely watch and wait for further developments? Bud was all for an immediate show-down with the linguist.

"Let's go see what's in that envelope," he urged.

"Bud, we have no right to pry into Hutchcraft's personal property."

"Well, at least let's go *look* at the envelope," Bud begged. "If he had anything to do with sabotaging the paraplane, we have a right to protect ourselves."

"Okay. We'll do some sleuthing."

The two boys, carrying flashlights, headed into the forest without telling anyone where they were going. The jungle lay shrouded in silence, broken occasionally by the eerie calls of night birds in the faint glow of moonlight.

Bud halted about a hundred yards from the digging site. "This is it," he said, focusing the beam of his flashlight on a crumbled slab of stone.

Tom lifted the stone a few inches and pulled out a bulky Manila envelope. He held it close to the light.

"There's nothing on it," Bud muttered.

"Wait a minute!" Tom scrutinized the envelope closely and rubbed it gently with his finger tips.

"Bud, I believe there are traces of chemicals on this. It might be invisible writing."

Bud whistled. "That does make it suspicious."

"Maybe we can bring the writing out," Tom replied. "I brought some chemicals from the *Sky Queen* to use in cleaning up those Mayan relics. They're still in the jeep."

"Okay, let's get 'em!" Bud urged.

The jeep was parked on the outskirts of the village, so the boys were able to secure the chemicals without being noticed. Tom hastily mixed a solution in a test tube. Then he moistened a wad of cotton and rubbed it over the envelope.

"Stealing your plans!" Bud gasped. "That's

The boys were thunderstruck as a series of words slowly appeared:

DRAWINGS OF TOM SWIFT JR.'S PARACHUTE PLANE
by WILSON HUTCHCRAFT

"Stolen plans!" Bud gasped. "So that's what the sneaking rat's been up to!"

Angrily Tom opened the envelope and pulled out a sheaf of large, folded papers. All seven were blank. Bud looked at his friend questioningly.

"More invisible writing?"

"Let's find out," Tom proposed quickly.

He daubed the sheets, one by one, with the chemical solution. It revealed diagrams of the entire electrical system of Tom's paraplane!

Bud was enraged. "That creep!" he cried out.

what the low-down sneak has been doing!"

"The skinny guy must be an accomplice!" Tom added. "Hutchcraft leaves the plans here for him to take!"

Tom hastily outlined a plan. After stuffing the papers into the envelope and replacing it under the stone, the two boys hurried back to the village. They found Hutchcraft lounging in the plaza.

"You seem all worked up, fellows." He grinned at them mockingly. "Don't tell me you've found another buried temple!"

"No, but we do have something to show you," Tom replied. "It's a secret. I'd like you to come and have a look—you may be able to help us."

Hutchcraft became intensely curious. His eyes gleamed with sudden interest. "Can't you tell me what it is?"

"We're not sure," Bud put in. "Come and see for yourself!"

The Bostonian needed no urging. Obviously intrigued by Tom and Bud's mysterious manner, Hutchcraft accompanied the boys eagerly. They led him into the forest and stopped beside the flat stone. Bud pointed to it. "Any idea what's under here, Hutchcraft?"

In the glow of their flashlights, the man's face went ash-white. "I . . . I don't know what you're talking about," he said nervously.

"Oh, no?" Tom reached under the stone and yanked out the envelope. "Suppose you explain this!"

Hutchcraft made an effort to pull himself together. "I tell you I know nothing about it!" he snarled. "You fellows are just trying to trap me into a phony confession—or—or something. Well, I don't have to stand here and listen to any trumped-up charges."

He tried to dart away, but Bud grabbed the linguist and swung him around angrily. "You've had this coming for a long time!" the copilot growled. His fist shot out and caught Hutchcraft squarely on the jaw.

He crumpled under the blow. With a moan he struggled to his feet as Bud stood over him with clenched fists.

"Don't hit me!" Hutchcraft begged. "I'll talk! Just don't hit me again!"

"All right. Make it snappy," Tom told him coldly.

"It's true, I *was* trying to steal the plans of your paraplane," Hutchcraft admitted. "But I didn't want to. A man named Felzer—Aaron Felzer—he made me do it."

"What do you mean—he made you do it?"

"I ran up some debts with him, and couldn't pay back the money," Hutchcraft explained. "He threatened to sue me, even have me thrown in jail, if I didn't help him. Felzer is a patent pirate. He learned you were inventing a new-type plane and figured that if he could get hold of the drawings, he could have them patented in his own name before you got your ship on the market."

"How come you sabotaged the paraplane?" Bud put in. "And don't tell us it wasn't you!"

"All right, I admit it!" Hutchcraft cringed. "I wanted to keep you fellows grounded here till I had a chance to draw up a complete set of sketches. I'm really an engineer, you see."

"An electronics expert, too?" Tom said accusingly.

Hutchcraft nodded. "I suppose you've guessed the rest. I decided I might as well make plans of your retroscope, too. That's how I happened to repair the short circuit in the electronic brain. I did it almost without thinking, while I was tracing out the wiring. And I was the one who took shells out of your rifle."

As Tom and Bud glared at the man contemptuously, Tom said, "Is Felzer a skinny guy?"

"Why—uh—yes. How do you know?"

"He's been seen around here. Where's he hiding?"

Hutchcraft hesitated. "Aaron lives in a jeep he keeps hidden in the jungle. He spies on me. I hate him. He's responsible for everything, the skunk! Please don't have me arrested! I've copied some other plans too. I'll show you where they're hidden if you'll let me off!"

"We're not promising anything," Tom retorted sharply. "Show us the plans first."

"All right," Hutchcraft agreed meekly. "Follow

me." He started off toward the excavation, with the boys close behind to prevent him from making a break. "The plans are hidden under some rocks on the other side of the diggings," the Bostonian explained.

"Did you help yourself to Max's treasures or was that Felzer?" Bud asked as they picked their way across the mound.

"I didn't do it, so it must have been Felzer," Hutchcraft insisted.

The three were now passing the cave-in where Tom and Bud had fallen into the Mayan tomb. Suddenly Hutchcraft whirled around and swung his flashlight viciously at Tom, hitting him on the side of the head. Stunned, the inventor pitched into Bud. The impact knocked the boys' flashlights from their hands. For a moment Tom and Bud teetered on the edge of the pit, clawing the air to regain their balance! The next second, they plummeted into the yawning hole!

As they tumbled headlong into the darkness below, they heard Hutchcraft laugh fiendishly. "Now this will be *your* tomb, too!" he shrieked. "And here's a grenade to make sure of it!"

CHAPTER XX

SPACEMEN'S FATE

HUTCHCRAFT'S threatening words echoed in the boys' ears as Tom and Bud landed, sprawling, on the floor of the tomb. An instant later they heard the grenade hit the floor beside them with a metallic clang!

"Quick! Out of the way, Tom!" Bud cried.

Both made a frantic leap to get out of range of the explosion, and hurled themselves flat. Tom was already counting under his breath: *"One . . . two . . . three . . . four . . ."*

He reached twenty and still nothing happened. "We're safe, Bud!" he muttered huskily. "Hutchcraft must have forgotten to pull the pin!"

The boys remained flattened a while longer to make sure the bomb or grenade was not a delayed-action type. Finally they got to their feet, still shaken from their close call.

"What a scare!" Bud gulped.

178

"But we're alive, pal—we're alive!" Tom drew a deep breath of relief!

"Now all we have to do is get out of here," Bud remarked dryly.

"Let's try shouting," Tom suggested.

Both boys yelled at the top of their lungs, together at first, then taking turns. At last they gave up, winded and hoarse.

"No use," Tom said. "The village is too far away. Looks as if we'll either have to wait for someone to show up or find our own way out."

"That'll be fun," Bud said gloomily.

The underground chamber was in inky darkness, except for the pale moonlight that barely shone down through the opening.

"There are two exits from this room," Tom mused, trying to visualize the layout. "I wonder where they go?"

Suddenly Bud snapped his fingers. "Tom! When the crew stopped digging today, I noticed something on the outside of the mound that looked like a door. It's still half covered, but we might be able to crash our way out—if we can find it."

Tom rummaged in his pockets and produced a ball of twine. "We can use this to lay a trail and keep our bearings," he suggested.

"Smart idea," Bud said. "Let me go first. I think I have a general idea which direction that door is located."

"Okay, but watch your step!" Tom tied the loose end of the twine to Bud's finger and held onto the ball himself.

Cautiously Bud groped through the darkness. To find the door, he knew he would first have to make contact with the wall, which in turn meant probably bumping into some of the skeletons. The very thought made Bud shudder.

Suddenly his foot kicked against something. There was a crash, as of bones clattering to the floor. "Good grief—I've done it!" Bud gulped.

Reaching out through the darkness, his fingers touched the wall. Bud felt his way along, inch by inch. Moments later, he came to a small archway. Going through it, he found himself at the foot of a stone stairway.

The steps were so narrow and steep he had to plant his feet sideways on them. At the top he found a narrow, winding corridor. After following this for about twenty feet, he discovered his progress blocked by what felt like a wooden door. Bud shoved, but the door refused to budge.

"Think I've found it, Tom!" he called out.

"Okay! Wait right there!" Tom called back. The young inventor laid down what was left of the ball of twine as a marker and began following the string. After knocking his shin against a stone statue and almost falling on his face when he stumbled against the stairway, Tom finally reached his friend.

"It's going to take some muscle to break this door open," Bud warned.

"Let's give it the old heave-ho!" Tom said. On signal, they crashed their shoulders against the ancient wooden door. It creaked, but did not move. Again they tried, without success.

The third crash brought a splintering sound. On their fourth attempt, the door finally burst open amid a shower of loose dirt and stones.

"Oh man, does that night air feel good!" Bud gulped.

"Guess we'll have to make it back to the village in the dark," Tom said. "At least we have a little moonlight to help us."

By following the truck and jeep tracks of the diggers, they finally reached the village. Here they poured out their story to Police Chief Rodriguez and the others. A hasty search was made for Hutchcraft, but a native reported that he had seen the linguist bundle up his gear and slip off into the jungle.

"Do not worry, señores," the police chief said. "I assure you he and his accomplice will not get far. My men and I will now take over!"

With Quetzal's help, Rodriguez hastily organized three search parties of native trackers. He, Pedro, and Miguel would each head a group.

Before the search parties could take off, however, there was an outburst of excitement from the chattering Mayas. Hutchcraft was walking forward, his head down. Behind him strode the jungle giant.

"It's Magnificent Max!" Bud cried.

Grinning broadly, the ex-wrestler came up into the firelight. In one huge hand he was holding a thin man like a kitten, by the scruff of his neck. In his other hand, Max was clutching a loaded knapsack and a sheaf of drawings.

"Here's your skinny guy and his pal!" Max boomed. "I knew I'd catch this sneak sometime!" Tom and the others cheered, with Max guffawing loudly, "I guess if this pip-squeak ain't scared o' the little men, I needn't be either!"

"Well done, Max!" Tom acclaimed him. "You even got back the plans of my inventions!"

"And in here's the stuff he stole from me!" Max went on, shaking the knapsack.

The thin man's face was livid with fear, but he tried to brazen his way out. "You fellows have no right to hold me!" he whined. "This is a frame-up!"

"No, it's not, Mr. Aaron Felzer," said Tom icily.

Luis Rodriguez snapped a pair of handcuffs on the man. "You and Mr. Hutchcraft will stand trial for assault, theft, and attempted murder!"

Both men started to argue but Ahau Quetzal silenced them, and remarked, "Now we can learn what the symbols say."

The next morning Tom and his assistants re-entered the tomb through the newly uncovered doorway. This time, they were amply provided with good lights and Tom brought a copy of the space dictionary.

He made his way down the stone steps into the burial chamber and immediately set about translating the wall inscriptions. After half an hour of work, he read off the translation to his companions:

" 'There are huge animals here which have killed several of us. We have tried to fly away but our . . . blank . . . will not work.' "

"What's the 'blank' for, boss?" Chow asked.

Tom sighed and frowned. "That's a symbol I can't figure out, Chow, even with the dictionary. It might be some kind of spaceship—or even something we've never heard of!"

The two sections of the new miniaturized camera were now lowered into the underground room through the opening in the top of the mound. Its electric cables extended to the computer and reproducer units, still aboard the truck. Tom trained the camera detectors on the wall, then switched on power. Moments later, Dick Folsom, who had remained topside, called down the reading which appeared on the time dial.

"Hold onto your hat, skipper!" he shouted. "Those symbols were carved around 1000 B.C.!"

"Wow!" Bud gasped. "Just think, Tom—those space friends of yours were advanced enough in science to make interplanetary voyages almost three thousand years ago!"

"My ancestors came here three thousand years ago?" Quetzal exclaimed.

"If they were ancestors, yes," Tom replied.

More photographing revealed that the warrior on the rocky wall had been carved much later—about A.D. 800. Tom said he thought the spacemen's carvings had been put on rocks out-of-doors. Later, they were considered sacred and a temple had been built around the symbols to preserve them. An excited discussion of the spacemen's probable fate followed. Had they perished, remained, or returned to their own planet?

Chow finally changed the subject. "Brand those jaguar whiskers, but I think the main point o' this whole expedition is that Tom's retroscope is a bang-up success."

Everyone cheered this statement, then Bud said, "Well, genius boy, what's next? More digging?"

"We'll leave this digging here to the archaeologists, Bud," Tom replied with a grin. "Right now, I'm eager to get back to Shopton and contact our space friends. I want to learn what *their* 'history books' have to say about a space armada that flew to the earth three thousand years ago!"

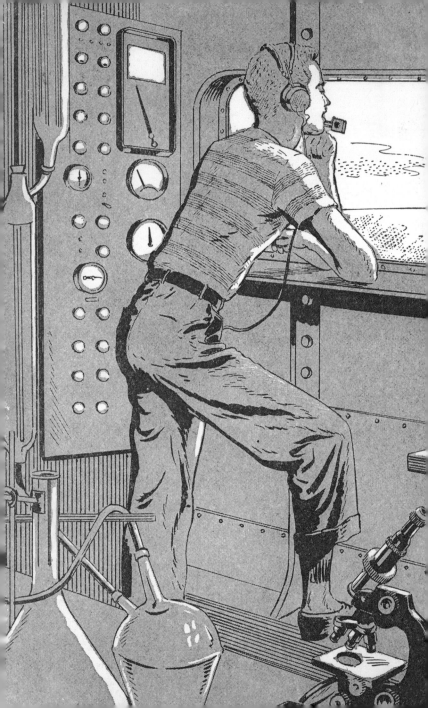